HIGH VOLTAGE
Lori Copeland

Author of More Than Six Million Books in Print!

A MODEST PROPOSAL

"Would you mind if I ask you to do me a big favor?" Laurel rushed on before she lost her nerve completely.

"I told you I'm doing everything within my power to help you with those turkeys." Clay sighed.

"I'm not talking about the farm. This is of a more personal nature....I've thought it through carefully and I'm convinced that you are the only logical one to help me with my problem."

"You have more *problems* than any one person I've ever met," he chuckled. "But go ahead and ask your favor."

She tried to find her voice but failed.

"Well?" Clay leaned over and tipped her face upward. "Laurel?"

Swallowing hard, she grinned weakly. "Would you be interested in having an affair with me?"

LORI COPELAND

HIGH VOLTAGE

LOVE SPELL ◆ NEW YORK CITY

LOVE SPELL®

January 1994

Published by

Dorchester Publishing Co., Inc.
276 Fifth Avenue
New York, NY 10001

Printed in the United States of America.

HIGH VOLTAGE

CHAPTER ONE

Paige Moyers was getting old.

The thin streak of hair perched on top of his head was snow-white. His face was weatherbeaten and wrinkled, and he looked tired most of the time now.

Eyes that were once a clear, arresting blue had grown faded with the passing of time . . . and it was sad.

". . . and I, Samuel Henderson, being of sound mind, do hereby declare all the rest of my entire estate, real, personal, or mixed, of whatsoever kind to my youngest daughter, Laurel. . . ."

The lawyer's voice droned on as one of the two young women sitting before his desk lifted startled green eyes in his direction.

Paige Moyers cleared his throat, then continued reading from the legal document he was holding in his hand.

"To my eldest daughter, Cecile, I leave the sum total of one dollar and the sincere wish that she will someday find what she is so desperately seeking."

A soft gasp escaped Laurel Henderson as she

turned to face her sister, a look of disbelief clearly evident on her stunned features. "I . . . Cecile, I had no idea. . . ."

The small, petite blonde facing her looked momentarily pained before she carefully pulled a cool mask of aloofness over her face. Shrugging her shoulders in mute acceptance, she reached for another cigarette from the crumpled package she had withdrawn from her purse earlier.

"It's only fair, Laurel. You were the one who stayed and helped run the farm, then took care of Dad through all the days of his illness," she pointed out. "And since he has never forgiven me for leaving him when I did, it comes as no surprise that he would disinherit me."

Laurel knew her father and Cecile had talked just prior to his death, and she had desperately hoped they had reconciled their differences.

Samuel Henderson had washed his hands of his eldest daughter years ago when she left for California amid his violent protests. Cecile had always been the daughter with big expectations and fanciful dreams. She wanted to be an actress, not a turkey farmer, and Samuel had never been able to understand her fantasies.

His wife had died giving birth to Laurel, and since then, he had worked hard at raising his two daughters to be doers, not daydreamers.

In the end Laurel had been the one to stay behind and help run the farm while Cecile chased her rainbows.

"But never once did he indicate that he was

leaving the farm to me," Laurel protested, her mind still trying to grasp the unexpected situation.

For years she had dreamed of the day when she could go on with her life. Not that she had resented caring for her father and running the farm after his stroke three years ago, but now he was gone and she was still young . . . still had time to start a new life.

"I . . . I don't *want* the farm." She moaned, half to herself, half to whoever would listen.

She had never wanted to stay and work the farm, let alone own it!

"Well"—Cecile lit her cigarette and blew a long white cloud of smoke indifferently toward the ceiling—"that seems rather immaterial. It's all yours now, lock, stock, and . . . turkey."

Laurel turned to the old family attorney, her eyes silently pleading for help. "Paige, does it have to be this way?"

She would be able to trust Paige's judgment in this matter. Oh, he had been growing increasingly forgetful lately. She sometimes had to remind him two or three times to do various things for her in the legal realm, but he was still a wise old person, and she would trust him with her life.

Paige sighed and lay Samuel Henderson's last will and testament back on his desk. "It's how your father wanted it. Of course, you could always sell the farm," he offered. "I know what a strain you've been under lately, and you could always move back to Kentucky. Doesn't Sam have a sister still living there?"

Laurel's face clouded with worry as she thought about the trouble she had been having recently.

Trying to run one of the largest turkey farms in the county had not been easy at best, and coupled with the suspicion that someone had been trying to run her out of business the last few months with acts of subversion and downright sabotage, Laurel had been kept awake many a night. Yes, she could sell the farm and play right into that person's hands, but she wouldn't.

"No, my father's sister passed away last year. But I wouldn't sell under pressure, anyway," she said firmly. "Dan and I have worked too hard to build the farm into what it is today. When I sell—*if* I sell—it will be because I want to, not because a bunch of hoodlums are trying to run me out of business!"

"You could always give Dan full control of running the farm," Paige suggested. "After all, he's been your foreman for the last five years and he knows turkeys like the back of his hand."

Without Dan Colburn's help Laurel knew she would never have made it the last few months, but Dan couldn't run the farm alone.

"No, that wouldn't work, either," she admitted.

"Then I'm afraid we've exhausted the choices . . . for now." Paige stood as Laurel and Cecile prepared to leave the office, his kindly eyes resting upon Laurel affectionately. "Give yourself some time to think about this calmly, dear. You've just been through a very trying time in your life, what with Sam's death and all the trouble you've been having out at the farm. It will be a while before the estate is settled. You might feel different about things in a few days. Selling the farm is really the only sensible thing for you to do now that Sam's gone."

"I don't know, Paige. I'm totally confused right now," she confessed.

Paige patted her shoulder reassuringly. "I'm sure you'll make the sensible choice when the time comes. You run along home now and get some rest. I'll be contacting you in a few days and we'll talk again."

Laurel drew a deep, defeated breath. A new life for Laurel Henderson would have to wait but not for very much longer. She was thirty-one years old. Time had a way of sneaking up and robbing a person of all their dreams if they weren't careful, and she didn't have much longer to tarry.

The heat of the hot July morning surrounded them as the two sisters left the lawyer's office each lost in her own thoughts.

For Laurel it was a disturbing, almost frightening time. Having the full responsibility of running the farm was a sobering realization, although, in truth, the responsibility had rested squarely on her shoulders the last few years.

Yet Samuel had always been around at the end of the day, and she would slip into his room to talk over the problems she had faced that day. The last few months, when her father's health had begun to fail rapidly, she would sit by his bedside and talk quietly. Only the occasional tightening of his hand in hers indicated that he had heard and understood her particular dilemma. At times she would lay her head on his broad chest and let the tears slip quietly down her cheeks. She knew the time was growing near when she would have no one to talk with, to love, to really care for, and a terrible sadness would wash over her.

All too soon that time had arrived.

For Cecile it was a numbing time.

Disinherited.

It was not only humiliating, it was frightening.

"You're terribly quiet for one who's just been handed a fortune," Cecile noted pensively.

"Oh, Cecile. There isn't any fortune. Dad and I have barely been able to make ends meet the last two years," Laurel revealed sadly. "With the extra money I've been sending you and the losses the farm has suffered lately, I'm afraid the only thing I've inherited is a pile of debts and one gigantic headache." Her footsteps faltered as they approached the older model pickup sitting at the curb, and she paused.

"Let's go have a cup of coffee before we go back to the farm," Laurel suggested impulsively. "I can't face reality yet."

"All right." Cecile's high heels tapped rhythmically on the hot sidewalk as she followed her sister toward the local café, quietly mulling over Laurel's words.

The farm nearly broke? That was news.

Moments later they were seated in a well-worn booth, achingly familiar to them both from their high school days. After placing their orders for coffee and sweet rolls, Cecile turned to her sister worriedly.

"Laurel, I had no idea you and Dad were in trouble financially. Why, the check you've sent me each month has been so generous, I thought everything was going fine."

"I know. I suppose I did get carried away, but I wanted you to have every chance to succeed," Laurel confessed, love and admiration for her sister shining in the depths of her eyes.

"Dad never knew you were sending me money, did he?" Cecile chided.

"No, but he had mellowed lately," Laurel defended, "and I know he loved you, Cecile. He . . . he was just sort of disappointed that you didn't want the things he did . . . didn't share his dreams. You know how bullheaded he could be at times. But I know he missed you and wanted you to come back home."

"I could tell by the will how much he loved and missed me," Cecile said sourly, reaching for her cigarettes.

"I was hoping you and Dad had made your peace before he died. I know you spent over an hour with him that last evening."

"I think we did, in our own way," Cecile said softly. "He was a tough old goat, but I loved him and I'm sorry I caused him the grief that I did. It's just . . . I didn't think he would really cut me out of his will."

Her eyes filled with tears for the first time since her father's death.

Laurel's eyes immediately filled with tears of

her own. "I'm as surprised by that as you are. Never once did he indicate that he had taken such drastic actions, but then, he never discussed his will with me." Leaning forward in the booth, she peered at Cecile intently. "You know whatever I have I will always share with you. We don't need a piece of paper to verify that, but I'm going to call Paige just as soon as I get home and have him draw up my will leaving you as soul beneficiary."

"You have always been too good for your own sake," Cecile scolded, and dabbed at her eyes guiltily. "I was the one who was chasing rainbows, while you actually had all the talent. But instead of complaining you stayed behind and helped Dad while I went out and made a fool of myself. How can you be so nice about it?"

"You didn't make a fool of yourself," Laurel said defensively. "You are a very talented actress. Maybe it just wasn't meant to be."

"I stunk as an actress, Laurel. Let's both face it and have done with it."

Laurel watched in mute commiseration as Cecile lit her cigarette and toyed with the matchbook. The pitiful look of defeat on Cecile's face nearly broke her heart. Cecile had tried. Lord knows, she had nearly killed herself for two years trying to get a start in acting, but she had failed miserably. She had come back home two weeks before Samuel's death, a sad, broken, but wiser person, only to face another crushing disappointment when her father disinherited her.

Yet she sat across from Laurel now, her striking good looks turning the heads of more than one of the men who sat in the café, and she smiled through a veil of tears.

"So, what about you?" Cecile asked. "I suppose after the estate is settled you will sell the farm and then go on with your music."

Laurel toyed with her napkin thoughtfully, her mind drawn to her love of the piano. After high school she had gone on to college to get a master's degree in music. But later, the farm demanded her time and she had set her career aside for the time being. It had always been her dream to go back to school for her doctorate someday.

But when Cecile left, Laurel had been forced to stay on the farm and help her father. Over the years she had played daily for her own and her father's enjoyment, visualizing the day when she could make her daydreams a reality.

Had the time come when she would finally be able to realize that dream?

"I don't know, Cecile. I would love to go on with my music, but I'll have to get the farm back on its feet before I can sell."

The waitress had brought their order, and Cecile was busy spreading butter over one of the mouthwatering cinnamon rolls before her. Reaching for the sugar bowl, she grinned sheepishly as she dumped three heaping teaspoons in her coffee cup. "Don't say a word! I haven't been able to do this for two long years, and if I'm not going to be the next Morgan Fairchild,

I'm certainly going to enjoy sugar in my coffee, and sweet rolls and butter once again!"

"Are you serious? I wouldn't say a word. I'm hoping you'll put on at least fifteen pounds and catch up with me!" Laurel exclaimed as she reached for her own roll.

"Gosh, these are as good as I remember them to be." Cecile sighed, licking the sticky icing off her fingers. "I used to dream about these things when I would wake up in the middle of the night so hungry, I could have eaten the paper off the walls."

"You're much too thin," Laurel assured her.

"I know, I had to be . . . but not anymore!" She signaled for the waitress to bring two more cinnamon rolls.

"We'll make ourselves sick." Laurel giggled.

"Who cares?"

Their relieved laughter broke the tension of the past few days. While they ate their second rolls at a more leisurely pace, Laurel filled her sister in on the strange happenings at the farm during the past few months.

"Well, can't the local authorities come up with a culprit?" Cecile demanded indignantly when her sister told of the hundred baby turkeys—poults, as they were referred to—that Dan had found dead that morning. "Who's the sheriff of the county now?"

"Clay Kerwin."

Cecile's mouth dropped open. "Our Clay Kerwin?"

"The same," Laurel revealed.

"Well, you certainly don't sound very happy about it. Don't you two get along nowadays?"

"Oh, sure, Clay and I get along, I guess." Laurel looked thoughtful for a moment. She had known Clay for as long as she could remember, and although they seemed to bicker a lot lately, she supposed she actually got along with him.

Granted, he had certainly gotten on her nerves at times with his complete lack of dedication to her problem at the farm.

And, considering his feelings toward her and the turkeys, they just might not get along much longer.

"I don't think he likes me anymore," she countered. "At least, he doesn't like my turkeys."

"For heaven's sake, why not?" Cecile leaned closer and whispered, "Is he still as tall, dark, and utterly male as he used to be?"

Laurel's face puckered pensively. "I don't know. I haven't noticed."

"Haven't noticed! Gad, have you got a turkey feather in your brain?" Cecile scoffed.

"No, I don't have a turkey feather in my brain. It just so happens that I'm too busy to notice what Clay Kerwin or any other man looks like at the moment."

"Then you're too busy," she dismissed airily. "I have always said, what you need is a good old blockbuster of a love affair with a dashing man who'll make you forget the conservative side of Laurel Henderson."

"That may be, but I haven't stumbled over such a paragon yet."

"Hmmm ..." Cecile munched contentedly. "Wonder if Clay's married yet?"

"No, he's not."

"Dating anyone seriously?"

"Are you asking out of curiosity or for future reference?"

Cecile shrugged. "It's worth thinking about, but I don't think he would be interested in me."

"Why not? I always thought he had a crush on you in school."

"*Me*? I thought he liked you!"

"*Me*?" They both stared at each other in disbelief. "What in the world makes you think he liked me?" Laurel choked out.

"Well, he was always hanging around both of us, and he sure didn't single me out to lavish his attention on."

"He didn't single me out, either," Laurel protested. "Oh, we used to hang around together some, and I suppose at one time I thought he was cute, but nothing serious ever went on between us."

"No kidding. Well, if he didn't really care for either one of us, I wonder why he always managed to show up wherever we happened to be?"

"I'm sure I don't know. But if he ever had a crush on me, he's over it now," Laurel said, laughing. "In fact, Clay and I barely speak when we see each other on the street nowadays, and if we do happen to have a conversation, we always end up in a fight."

Laurel was well aware that with Clay's dark good looks, he was the town's most eligible bachelor, and nothing prevented him from having female companionship. And Laurel was sure he had never paid her the slightest bit of attention since he graduated from high school.

In fact, the last time he had singled her out to say anything remotely personal to her, it had made her blood boil.

She remembered the occasion as if it had been yesterday.

It was last fourth of July, and she could still feel the heat of the day bearing down on her back as she stood in the lemonade stand dipping out the cold, icy glasses for the Ladies Auxiliary fund-raiser at the town's annual picnic.

Sheriff Kerwin had sauntered by her booth with his deputy, Buck Gordon, and they had paused to purchase a glass of the fruity drink.

Exhibiting every bit of his Indian heritage, Clay was indeed a handsome man. Jet-black hair and dark olive skin, combined with his six-foot two-inch, two-hundred-twenty-five-pound frame made for an imposing sight for all who looked upon him.

Only the brilliant blue of his eyes belied his full lineage. His mother had been an beautiful full blooded Cherokee Indian who had fallen head over heels in love with Clay's father, a tall, handsome Irishman.

Yes, Laurel had to admit he was a heartbreaker. Not only that, he was tough.

For years the county had suffered under the administration of a corrupt sheriff. When Clay Kerwin ran for office, he had promised to clean up the town and make it once again a reputable, law-abiding place to live. He had been in office only a couple of years, but his reputation for keeping his campaign promise was spreading fast.

He could be ruthless without batting an eye if the occasion called for it, but he was also known for having an unusual sense of justice and fair play about him. Day by day he was returning the county to what it had once been.

"Afternoon, Laurel."

Buck Gordon had smiled politely as he handed her a dollar bill, and in return she handed him two glasses of lemonade.

"It's shore a hot one today," he observed, wiping the sweat off his brow with a large white handkerchief.

"It certainly is." Laurel glanced at Clay and smiled pleasantly. "Hi, Clay."

"Hi, Laurel."

The brief flash of even, white teeth caught her eye as she busied herself squeezing more lemons. For some crazy reason she caught herself wondering why she had never noticed how broad his shoulders had become in the last few years.

Shrugging the disturbing image away, she tossed the lemon rinds in the waste can and poured two additional glasses for the older couple who had walked up to the window. They stood chatting for a few minutes exchanging idle pleasantries with the sheriff and his deputy.

When the three wandered away a few minutes later, Clay lagged behind, holding out his glass for a refill.

Laurel had felt an unusual shyness come over her as she poured the liquid in the glass, avoiding his vivid blue gaze.

She was horrified a few seconds later when she looked down to see the glass running over and the sticky sweet lemonade dripping down the cuff of his uniform shirt.

"Oh, my ... how clumsy of me," she murmured, and grabbed a towel to mop up the dripping remains.

Glancing at his wet sleeve, he frowned, then, after picking a lemon seed off, excused her graciously before he made another attempt at conversation.

"Looks like it might rain before evening," he commented. He leaned his large frame against the edge of the stand and looked off into the distance where large thunderheads were beginning to gather.

Laurel caught the faint scent of soap and a clean-smelling after-shave as a refreshing breeze sprang up.

"Yes, it looks like it could."

"How's the turkey business?" he asked idly.

"Busy." She stiffened at the mention of her business. She knew full well Clay would love to see her and her turkeys driven out of town.

"You know," he continued conversationally, "it's a crying shame to litter our nice little town with all those unsightly turkey feathers."

Laurel frowned. Oh, brother. He was going to start *that* again!

She turned her coolest green gaze in his direction.

"I'm very sorry my turkeys are hindering your plans to make this town a tourist attraction, but really Sheriff Kerwin, do you honestly think my turkey feathers bother anyone in this town but *you?*" She gave him her snootiest look. "Has anyone complained?"

"No, they haven't complained . . . yet." He turned his nose right back up at her in that infuriating way he could when he was trying to irritate her. "But they're bound to when they wake up some morning and they're buried in the damn things. Now, if you could just find it in your heart to reroute the transportation of those turkeys off the main road leading into town, you'll save us both a lot of trouble—" he reasoned patiently.

"I can't do that. I transport my turkeys by the quickest, most economical route I can find," she interrupted curtly. "And that happens to be the main road."

His blue gaze narrowed in warning.

"Then I suggest, Laurel Henderson, for the benefit of your community, you think about a new route. I, for one, am tired of turkey feathers flyin' around my car as I'm driving down the highway every day. So, I'm quite sure"—he held up one finger to help stress his point—"even though they don't say anything about it, it gets on other people's nerves too," he said in a bristly tone.

"Then they'll just have to look the other direction when they drive through town," she snapped. "I have every right to transport my turkeys the way I see fit!"

"Not if it's hurting the town, you don't," he snapped back.

"Not one other person has *ever* mentioned my turkey feathers," she defended hotly. "Just because you want to play big shot and clean up the town does not mean you can start telling people how to run their businesses. I am a law-abiding citizen who's making an honest living. Go take a hike, Clay Kerwin!"

Clay jerked his hands back quickly as she slammed the window down in his face angrily.

"You better give serious thought to my suggestion," she heard him shout through the wooden cracks. "I'm getting fed up with those damn turkeys, and I'm going to haul you in and fine you for littering if you mess around with me!"

"I wouldn't 'mess around' with you if my life depended on it," she shot back in a snide tone, and left the booth in a mad huff.

From that day on they had both been coolly polite to each other when they passed on the street. Thank heavens he hadn't carried through on his threat to fine her . . . yet.

When the trouble started at the ranch a few months ago, she hesitated about calling him. But after finding nearly five hundred turkeys dead in one of the grow-out houses one day, she was forced to turn to Sheriff Kerwin for his help, even though it nearly killed her.

She had no delusions that he would be overly sympathetic to her cause.

He wanted those turkeys out of town, and he made no bones about it.

"Hey, where did you go?"

Cecile's voice brought her abruptly back to the present as she realized she had been reliving the last few months and her strained association with Clay.

"Oh, I was just thinking," Laurel explained lamely.

"About the turkeys?"

"Yeah, about one *great* big one," she acknowledged with an impish grin.

CHAPTER TWO

It was downright hot.

Not the moist, sultry warmth that had teased the town for all of June, but the kind of stifling July heat that surrounds a man and makes him cranky and irritable and long for cooler days.

Sheriff Clay Kerwin stood in his office and stared out the large picture window behind his desk.

Lately this room had been as much his home as the rambling two-story house sitting on twenty acres on the outskirts of town.

The concrete walls were lined with his certificates of accomplishments in the field of law enforcement, assuring the small town that they had made a wise choice in their selection of Clay Kerwin.

Although Clay was careful to hide his feelings, he couldn't help but swell with pride when he thought about the things he had managed to achieve during his short time in office.

One of the largest marijuana rings in the Midwest had been disbanded, the majority of corrupt officials in the town had been run out of office, and with a little more time, the rest would follow.

Clay loved this town and its people.

For ten years prior to his election, he had worked as a deputy under the dishonorable leadership of the former sheriff, Burl Mason. Clay's strong sense of right and wrong had warred constantly within him as he stood silently by and watched the town being victimized by a man who was nothing more than a small-time gangster. When the time came that he could no longer stand idly by and watch the town being terrorized, he resigned from his job and announced his intentions to run for sheriff in the following election.

It had been a tough and sometimes dirty campaign, fraught with deceit and lies. Sheriff Burl Mason had done everything within his considerable power to assure Clay's defeat, but the people of this small town in Arkansas had finally found some backbone. They turned out in record numbers to vote Clay into office with a landslide victory.

Touched by their overwhelming support, Clay made a silent vow he would never do anything to lose the trust the town had placed in him.

So, one of his dreams had been realized, and the other ... Clay sighed as his eyes fastened on the auburn-haired woman who just walking out of the local café with her sister.

And the other, his thoughts continued longingly, the other dream would never be realized, and he had better start getting that through his thick skull.

Laurel Henderson.

For one tantalizing moment Clay let his gaze linger on the slender figure walking to the red pickup parked in front of the café, his eyes hungrily surveying her graceful movements.

A slight breeze lifted her hair off her shoulders and tossed it gently around delicate features. Although he couldn't see them, he knew her eyes were a clear, arresting green, sometimes sparkling with mischief, sometimes with laughter, sometimes with anger . . . *most* of the time with anger when she was around him, he granted with an indignant snort.

He had fallen in love with Laurel Henderson the first time he had seen her on the schoolground when he was in the seventh grade.

Clay was not a person prone to instant attraction, but when he glanced up and saw her standing shyly in the background, her expressive eyes quietly assessing the multitude of strangers, his heart went out to her. It wasn't so long ago that he had been the stranger, moving to town a year earlier with his parents and two brothers.

Only for him, the move had been much harder.

With a full-blooded Indian mother and a giant of an Irishman for a father, he had taken a lot of teasing from the other children.

Little Indian boy, the children taunted, dancing around him amid loud bellows of war whoops. Blue-eyed half-breed . . . half-pint savage; they had thought of all the names that could hurt and tear through his heart and make him long to go home and hide.

But Clay was never one to run away from trouble, and soon, with the aid of his fist and some very pointed and unsavory name-calling of his own, he gradually made a place for himself. The other kids steadily came to admire and respect him—all except the one whose attention he had tried so hard to capture.

Laurel had always looked on Clay, in his opinion, as just . . . good old Clay.

He had attributed it to her being a bit stuck-up.

She always had to hurry home from school to practice her piano while the other kids her age gathered down at the local drugstore for Cokes and french fries. On occasion her sister Cecile had talked Laurel into letting go and enjoying life for a few hours. But on those occasions Laurel usually paired off with Marsh Cranston, the heartthrob of Burnsville High and a gigantic pain in the butt to the boys of the town who tried to keep a steady girl friend.

When Clay got his first car, he had tried hard to impress Laurel with his driving expertise by squealing his tires around the corner, making her jump back with fright as she and Marsh walked home from school one afternoon.

He was reasonably sure he would have impressed her, too, if one of the tires hadn't blown out and nearly caused him to turn the car upside down.

Instead he had wiped out one whole block of

a white picket fence and overturned the town's only statue, which sat in the middle of the square, killing four pigeons and a sparrow that was roosting on it.

Needless to say, she wasn't the least bit impressed.

There had been a lot of Saturday afternoons when he'd squired the Henderson sisters around town in his car, but Laurel had never paid much attention to him.

His eyes darkened as a recurring memory cropped up again in his mind.

At least he had been the first man to ever kiss Laurel Henderson. It had been a stolen kiss and one she had only laughed at, but it had been his and his alone.

He grinned smugly.

He had learned a thing or two about kissing since then, and he would give his eyeteeth to have that opportunity again.

Yes, it wouldn't be a young boy's kiss, and he'd bet his last dollar she wouldn't walk away laughing this time. . . .

Clay blushed now as he thought back to his childish antics and how miserably he had failed to impress her.

Funny.

They neither one had married yet. Actually he knew Laurel hadn't had the time to marry. She was so busy running that damn turkey farm, she rarely socialized.

He told himself he had never married because he had never found the time, either, but deep down he knew the real reason.

He had never found a girl he wanted to marry other than stuck-up Laurel Henderson, and she certainly wasn't interested in him.

He would die before he let her know he still harbored a crush for her even after all these years. No, after his disastrous teenage years of trying to attract her attention he had taken special precautions against her ever even suspecting that he, Clay Kerwin, cared one little whit for her!

Just let her end up a wrinkled old maid on that damn turkey farm!

It would serve her right as far as he was concerned. She barely had a civil word for him when she passed him on the street, he fumed. Her and her confounded temper!

It seemed the only conversations they had always ended up in some sort of petty squabble. Laurel was sure Clay wasn't doing enough to catch the people responsible for intimidating her. On the other hand, Clay felt he was doing all he could and was growing increasingly tired of Laurel's accusations.

And he would bet his last dime she wouldn't leave town this morning without coming over to nag him again about "how little he was doing"!

Clay shifted his weight uneasily and watched the two sisters exchange a few short words before Cecile started toward the drugstore and Laurel proceeded down the street in the direction of the jail.

Here she comes!

He'd hide. That was the coward's way out, but what the hell. He was in no mood for a hassle with her this morning. If he hurried; he could duck out the back door and she would never be the wiser.

Tiptoeing backward across the room, he kept his eyes fixed on the front door as he crept silently past the cells and out the back door. Quietly pulling the door closed behind him, he turned and came face-to-face with flashing green eyes.

"Good morning, Sheriff Kerwin," a familiar feminine voice purred sweetly.

"Uh . . . Laurel." He grinned guiltily. "Good morning!"

"Going somewhere?" she asked pleasantly, but he could tell by the look in her eye that she knew exactly what he was doing.

"Just taking the trash out," he shot back defensively.

They both looked at his empty hands.

"A few minutes ago. I took it out a few minutes ago," he clarified sheepishly.

Reaching out, he took her arm and steered her back into the jailhouse before she could contradict him.

"Take your hands off me, Clay Kerwin," she said, irritably shaking loose of his grip. "You were sneaking out that back door because you saw me coming, now, weren't you!" she accused.

"Who, me?" he gasped innocently.

"Yes, you!" Laurel reiterated.

"I was not," he lied. "Do you think I have nothing better to do than hide from you?"

Her face grew defiant. "I don't know what you do all day. I *do* know you certainly aren't out catching the imbeciles who are destroying my farm!"

"Now wait a minute!" His eyes were the ones growing defiant now. "You're not going to waltz in here and start throwing your weight around and telling me I'm not doing my job again—"

She stopped him before he could continue. "Tell me, Clay, are you aware that someone cut the power to the brooder house last night?" she asked curtly.

"Yes, Dan stopped by here first thing this—"

"Are you also aware that I lost close to three hundred poults because of that power failure?" she continued, knowing full well that her foreman had already reported the incident.

"He mentioned that, and Buck's out there right now checking on things," he returned stiffly.

"I don't understand this," Laurel cried in exasperation, starting to pace the floor. "*Why?* Why would anyone want to run me out of business? It simply doesn't make sense. Everyone loved Sam Henderson. To my knowledge my father never made an enemy in his life. So why all of a sudden is someone trying to kill off all our turkeys and force me to sell the farm?" Her pacing increased in intensity. "It couldn't be for the value of the land. It isn't that valuable. Why, when we moved here years ago we bought that forty acres dirt cheap. If it weren't for the turkeys, it wouldn't be worth a hill of beans to this day!"

"Those turkeys aren't worth a hill of beans if you ask me," he grumbled under his breath as he walked over to pour himself a cup of coffee.

"And just who asked you," she demanded, whirling to face him once more. "And don't you dare start bad-mouthin' my turkeys again this morning!" Her eyes narrowed in suspicion. "You know, I wouldn't put it past you to be in on this. You never have liked my turkeys, have you?"

"No, I haven't," he returned promptly. "And you want to know why?" Before she could answer, he told her. "I hate those damn feathers all over the roadside! I have feathers on my windshield, feathers in my car grille, feathers stuck on my boots! There's feathers in the grass, feathers in the trees, feathers in the bushes, feathers in the flowers. Just what do you think people passing through our town think?" he demanded irritably. "This is a pretty town, and your turkey feathers are driving me nuts!"

"I knew it. You hate my turkeys," she accused with a quivering lower lip.

"I hate their feathers *and* their smell," he agreed bluntly, without so much as blinking an eye, "but I'm not trying to run you out of business, so you can just get that idea out of your head right now. I'm doing all I can to find out who is, but you're just going to have to ride this thing out until I do."

"You're standing there calmly drinking coffee, telling me I have to 'ride this thing out' while someone is systematically killing my stock and financially ruining me?"

Her voice began to rise in hysteria as the strain of the past few weeks overtook her, and the temper Clay knew so well finally surfaced full strength.

"Well, it's just not enough!" To emphasize her point she snatched up one of the empty cups sitting beside the coffee urn and threw it at his feet, shattering the china into a million tiny pieces.

Without batting an eyelash Clay calmly took another sip of his coffee and completely ignored her tantrum.

If he had shouted at her or been angry about the broken cup, she would probably have apologized and cooled down. If he had been anything but the infuriating, cool man he was so perfect at being, she most assuredly would never have picked up the remaining cups and angrily bombarded his feet with them until he was standing in a pile of broken coffee cups, his blue eyes aloofly inspecting the mounting bits of china.

Taking one final sip of his coffee, he handed her the last cup and watched as she smashed that at his feet too.

"Well," he said matter-of-factly, as he crunched his way over to his desk and sat down. "Now that we've got all that out of our system, do we want to talk about this calmly?"

"You really irritate me, are you aware of that?"

"No kidding. And you were doing such a

good job of hiding it," he returned dryly. He leaned back in his chair and stretched his long legs out on the desk in front of him.

Her temper subsided as quickly as it had risen, and she sank down wearily in the chair facing his desk. For the first time Clay noted the signs of strain on her face, and he softened immediately. "Hey, look. I'm sorry if I irritate you, okay? Will you let me get you a cup of coffee and let's talk this thing over sensibly?"

"Oh, Clay, I don't know how much longer I can go on like this," she confessed, wiping at the gathering tears in her eyes. "These past few weeks have been a nightmare."

Clay walked over to a closet where he found a paper cup, then filled it with coffee, giving her a few moments to compose herself before they continued the conversation.

"I was sorry to hear about Sam's death," he offered gently. "I didn't get to speak with you the day of the funeral, but I wanted you to know that I thought a lot of your father. He was a good man."

"He always thought a lot of you and your family," Laurel conceded.

She took the cup he offered and held it between trembling hands, silently recalling Sam's words when Clay had been elected sheriff. "That boy will clean this town up, you mark my words," he had said with a broad grin. "He's tough enough to lay down the law and big enough to see that it's carried out."

Laurel's eyes involuntarily crept over to linger for a moment on Clay's impressive masculine physique.

He *was* big enough to enforce the law, she decided.

He had to be at least six-two or six-three, and she couldn't begin to guess his weight. There wasn't an ounce of fat on him, that was certain. Only a solid wall of muscle confronted her as he walked around the desk and took his seat again.

For the first time she really did wonder why Clay had never married. He was certainly good-looking enough to attract any woman he wanted.

When had he grown from that lanky, gawky Clay Kerwin she'd gone to school with into this virile, strikingly attractive man?

"How's your family?" Laurel asked politely.

"Mom's not doing too well, but Dad's going strong."

"What about Trigg and Sloan? It doesn't seem like I've seen your brothers around much lately."

"Trigg's been helping Dad out on the farm, and, of course, Sloan and Becky are busy with the new baby." Clay picked up a pencil and rolled it around between his thumbs. It felt strange to be sitting here carrying on a normal conversation with Laurel Henderson.

"A girl, wasn't it?"

"Yeah. She's a cute little dickens," he said, grinning shyly. "Nicole Rochelle . . . that's her name."

"That's nice. I suppose they'll call her Nikki?"

"Probably. Why do people do that?" he mused

thoughtfully. "Name a baby one thing, then call it something else."

Laurel shrugged. "Nicknames."

"How long is Cecile going to stick around town?" Clay asked, changing the subject. He reached into his pocket for a stick of gum. "You want a piece?" he offered.

"No, thanks."

"I quit smoking and started chewing," he confessed as he unwrapped the stick of gum and popped it in his mouth.

"I really don't know how long she'll be here," Laurel replied. "I hope she stays for a while, at least until I can get on my feet again and sell the farm."

"Sell the farm?" Clay's face suddenly lost its good humor. "I wasn't aware you'd put the farm up for sale."

"I haven't yet," she said, frowning. "But I'll have to before very long if I keep taking the losses I've been taking. We'd been just barely getting by before all the vandalism started, and now . . ."

"I've told you I'll take care of that," Clay said impatiently. "You're going to have to give me a little time, Laurel."

"It isn't only the vandalism, Clay. I *want* to sell the farm."

Clay's face hardened. "What does Cecile think about that?"

"It doesn't matter what Cecile thinks," she murmured. "It's up to me whether I sell or not."

"Now that Sam's dead, half of the farm is

hers, isn't it?" he pressed in a tightly controlled voice.

"No. Sam left everything to me," she returned quietly.

"To you?" He looked clearly puzzled.

"Yes, and don't ask why. I don't really understand why myself."

"How did Cecile take the news? She couldn't have been too happy," he observed tautly. He pushed back from the desk and started pacing the floor.

Laurel glanced up at him. "Why does that upset you so?"

She'd always suspected Clay had a crush on Cecile when they were in high school.

Although he never actually dated her sister, he had always been underfoot during those years. Maybe that's why he's never married, she thought fleetingly.

Maybe he was waiting around till Cecile came back, hoping . . .

"It doesn't upset me," he denied quickly, too quickly in Laurel's opinion. "I'm just surprised to hear that Sam would do that."

"Well, he did, and I'm sure I'm as surprised as everyone else is going to be," she admitted. "But as soon as I can, I'm going to sell the farm, split the money with her, and go on with my music. I'm sick of turkey farming."

"You're going back to school?"

"Yes, I want to get my doctorate and then teach."

A wistful look crossed his features now as he

turned to face the window, trying to let the news sink in.

Laurel would finally be leaving town.

"That's what you've always wanted, isn't it?" he queried softly.

"I think so. That's always been my dream. To be honest, I really don't know what I want, Clay," she confessed. "It just seems to me that I'm missing out on something in life. And before I'm too old to enjoy it, I want to have a chance to find out what it is I'm missing out on, if that makes any sense at all."

He turned from the window slowly. "I think you'll find you haven't missed out on a thing," he cautioned, "but I promise I'll do everything within my power to help you realize your dream."

"You mean, you'll work harder on my case." She brightened.

"I've been working as hard as I can, but I'll work harder," he promised in a tired voice.

"Oh, good!" Laurel stood up to leave, her spirits lifted considerably.

Clay wasn't such a bad guy, now that she stopped to think about it.

With his firm promise to bring the criminals to swift justice, she knew it wouldn't be long now before she could get on with her life.

Feeling a great deal more benevolent toward the county sheriff than when she first entered the office, she suddenly had an idea.

If he could be nice, so could she.

"Clay, do you have any plans for dinner this evening?" she asked impetuously.

Clay lifted his blue eyes in her direction. "No . . . why?"

"Good! Why don't you come by the house and have dinner with Cecile and me. You haven't seen her since she got back, have you?"

A glimmer of disbelief, then undisguised elation flooded his face. "No, I've seen her on the street, but . . ."

"Well, that's not good enough," Laurel said firmly. "I'm sure she would be delighted to see you again. Can you be there by about six thirty?"

"Sure," he agreed hurriedly, hardly daring to believe what was happening.

He knew he shouldn't be acting like a love-starved puppy, but Laurel Henderson was actually inviting *him* to have dinner with her.

"What's your favorite pie?"

"Mine? Uh . . ." He couldn't think straight, so he said the first thing thing that popped in his head, "Gooseberry," then instantly regretted his poor choice.

He not only disliked gooseberries with a passion, they also gave him heartburn for three days after eating them.

Laurel's face fell. Now why in the world did she mention pie? She was the world's worst pie baker!

"Oh, uh . . . gooseberry," she stammered. "Why, I believe that's Cecile's favorite too. Isn't that nice!"

Clay stared at her in bewilderment. He didn't care what kind of pie Cecile liked.

"Yeah, that's real nice." He nodded.

"Then we'll be expecting you around six

thirty," she said brightly, walking toward the front door.

She was going to have to dig up some gooseberries somewhere!

Clay trailed along behind her, still half-expecting her to retract the impulsive invitation.

"Can I bring anything?" he asked politely, as they reached the door.

"Just a big appetite." Laurel grinned.

He grinned back. "No problem there."

"Then we're all set." She turned to leave, then paused and turned back around. "Oh . . . and Clay. Thanks."

She stood on tiptoe and brushed his cheek briefly with a featherlike kiss.

For a moment he was so stunned by her actions, he froze. A few seconds later he felt his knees start to buckle and he was instantly put out with himself. Damn! A grown man who's kissed almost every girl in the county about to fall on his face all because Laurel Henderson gives him one impassioned kiss on the cheek!

Laurel was out the door before he could say anything, leaving only the faint trace of her perfume to indicate that she had ever been there.

Clay's hand came up to touch his cheek reverently, the blue of his eyes growing deeper. Now, why in hell had she done that, he mused painfully.

After all these years of either ignoring him or else fighting with him at every opportunity, she finally decides to acknowledge that he's alive—just before she sells the farm and moves off somewhere where he'll probably never see her again.

Giving the wall a vicious whack, he straightened up and walked back to his desk.

In a way he wished he'd never accepted her dinner invitation. Why make things harder than they already were?

But he knew he would go. Wild horses couldn't keep him away from an evening with Laurel Henderson, even if he did despise gooseberries with a burning passion.

With a boyish grin he went back to his desk and sat down, chewing on his gum happily.

Moments later he had blown the all-time biggest bubble of his gum-chewing career.

Dinner with Laurel Henderson . . . *his* Laurel Henderson.

Now, who ever would have believed that!

CHAPTER THREE

"Gad, am I glad you're home!"

Laurel let herself in the back door of the kitchen and dropped her bundle on the table in relief.

Cecile glanced up from polishing her long, perfectly shaped nails and laughed. "Where have you been?"

"Looking all over town for gooseberries. Do you know that old Mrs. Higgins was the only person in town who picked gooseberries this year?"

"Why did you bother? We hate gooseberries." Cecile went back to painting her fingernails.

"No, you don't. You *love* gooseberry pie." Laurel grinned. "And so does Clay Kerwin."

Cecile looked up at her blankly.

"I've invited Clay to dinner," Laurel said brightly, as she began to put away the groceries. "I figured you've had such a rotten day, what with the will and everything, that you needed some cheering up. If Clay did have a crush on you in school, now's his perfect opportunity to do something about it."

"You did!" Cecile perked up instantly and started blowing her nails dry. "Well, why didn't you tell me earlier," she scolded. "I have to wash my hair and pick out something decent to wear. Goodness, I don't have a single thing that looks good on me."

"With all the clothes you have in your closet you can't find one dress that looks good on you?" Laurel teased.

"I really can't. Is it going to be just the three of us?" Cecile questioned expectantly.

"I've been thinking about that. Maybe I should ask Dan too. What do you think?"

"Dan Colburn? Yes, I think you should. That way we could sort of pair off. I know Dan has a thing for you," she teased.

Laurel blushed.

She feared Dan "had a thing" for her too. She was only sorry she didn't return his admiration.

Oh, she liked Dan a lot, but not enough to marry him, and she hoped he'd never ask, so that she wouldn't have to hurt his feelings.

"That's what I'll do, then. I'll call Dan right away."

"Just remember, I've got first dibs on Clay for the evening," Cecile reminded her sister. "Funny, I never thought that much about him when we were in school, but now . . . well, it's sort of exciting," she admitted.

"That's why I invited him," Laurel announced.

"Do you still have that plum-colored sun dress I used to love so well?" Cecile asked.

"Yeah, but I sort of thought I might wear it myself," Laurel protested.

For some crazy reason all the way home she kept thinking she wanted to dress up special tonight, in Clay's honor.

She knew she was being downright silly. She had asked Clay here tonight so that he and Cecile could be together. And Dan would compliment her no matter what she wore, so why should she go to a lot of fuss?

"Oh, can't you wear something else?" Cecile pleaded. "That color is absolutely perfect for me."

"All right. I'll wear the salmon-colored one," she conceded in a grumpy voice.

"Great, that one looks better on you, anyway," Cecile complimented hurriedly, and started to scurry out of the room.

"Hey! Wait a minute!" Laurel pulled her back by the scruff of her collar.

"Laurel. I have a million things to do before Clay gets here," Cecile protested.

"And I do too," her sister informed her. "I'll prepare all of the dinner if you'll make the pie. Do you know how to make a gooseberry pie?"

Cecile grimaced. "Do I look like I know how to make a gooseberry pie?"

"No, but you're going to have to learn because I sure don't."

"But I'm a hideous cook, Laurel. You know that. I can't even boil water and make it turn out right," she wailed.

"There's no time like the present to start learning, Cecile. I'm sure you'll survive."

"I might survive, but it's the men I'm worried about," Cecile grumbled pitifully. "Gooseberry pie. That word *gooseberry* is ludicrous. Who ever named it that?"

"The same person who thought up the words *pussywillow* and *corkscrew*," Laurel guessed offhandedly. They both giggled. "You'd better drag out a cookbook to figure out how to make one, though, and it had better be good if you want to impress Clay Kerwin. It's his favorite pie."

"I couldn't impress anyone with my cooking! I'll do it only on the condition that the men think you've baked it," she bargained stubbornly.

"Cecile!"

"I mean it. I won't be embarrassed by my horrible cooking."

Laurel sighed and tied an apron around her waist. "All right. We won't say anything about you baking the pie, but what happens if it turns out mouthwatering and Clay praises it to high heavens?"

"Then, of course, I baked it," she relented.

Cecile was still moaning about her fate as Laurel went to the phone to call her foreman to ask him to dinner.

Laurel glanced at the others at the table and tried to keep her eyes from rolling around in her head.

This stinkin' gooseberry pie tasted like it didn't have a drop of sugar in it.

The dinner had gone well up till now, with

48

both men praising the fried chicken, cream gravy, and flaky biscuits Laurel had set before them.

She had accepted their compliments with just a touch of pink in her already rosy cheeks, taking pride in the fact that she was a good cook of anything but desserts.

It was a miracle she had gotten the meal together at all.

She had had to work around Cecile, who was groaning and carrying on as if the world were coming to an end. She was frantically trying to get the pie dough rolled out into some semblance of order.

It was finally placed in broken sections in the pie pan, the remaining ingredients dumped in on top.

I only hope it will taste better than it looks, Laurel thought as she struggled to get the kitchen window open.

While Cecile was upstairs putting on Laurel's plum-colored dress, the pie had run over in the oven. Pieces of dough were dropping through the racks, sending out a steady stream of black smoke from the oven.

The house still smelled as if it had burned to the ground.

Trying to keep the tears from streaming down her cheeks. Laurel pasted on a bright smile and asked in a perfect hostess voice, "More pie anyone?"

Clay swallowed hard and bit down on both sides of his cheeks, praying his jaws hadn't locked on him permanently.

"Uh . . . thanks, I think this is about gonna do me."

He hated gooseberry anything, let alone this sour concoction Cecile had placed before him. But if Laurel had baked it, he was bound and determined to eat it even if it killed him.

Laurel smiled and turned to Dan. "What about you, Dan?"

"Uh . . . no, no, I think I've had my share," he refused hurriedly, patting his slightly protruding stomach to prove that he was telling the truth.

"It sure is good. A bit tart but good!"

Tart! That was the understatement of the year!

"My!" Laurel exclaimed brightly, forcing another forkful of pie into her mouth. "I believe I should have added a tiny bit more sugar."

She winced painfully as she tried to swallow the exceedingly sour mixture.

"Do you remember how much sugar I put in this pie, Cecile?" she inquired pleasantly.

She shot a scathing look in her sister's direction.

Cecile had pushed her pie aside after the first bite, claiming that she was on a diet and simply *had* to watch every bite that was put in her mouth.

"Sugar? I don't recall *you* putting any sugar in the pie," Cecile hedged nervously.

"No sugar? I didn't put any sugar in this gooseberry pie?" Laurel asked incredulously.

Cecile was dumber than she had thought. No

sugar in a gooseberry pie. This was humiliating, to put it mildly.

"None?"

"Uh-uh."

Laurel kicked at Cecile's shins under the table. It was an old trick from their childhood days and was pretty effective in making a point.

Clay's eyes widened as Laurel missed her target and the point of her shoe dug into his leg painfully.

"Ouch!"

Cecile and Dan glanced at him expectantly.

"Sorry, I burned my tongue," he explained sheepishly.

Laurel leaned over and whispered her apology. "I'm sorry, my foot slipped."

He smiled nicely. "That's all right."

But his look told her he thought she was off her rocker.

All three began spooning their pie back in their mouths quietly.

"Laurel baked the pie," Cecile just had to add. "Isn't she a marvelous pastry cook?"

Once again Laurel took aim. She was really going to let her have it this time. But Cecile knew her sister's tricks, and she rose from the table at the same time Laurel let her foot fly.

"More coffee anyone?" Cecile asked.

Clay's fork clattered to the table as Laurel's foot struck his shin again.

Dan and Cecile whirled in his direction as he grinned weakly and shot Laurel a murderous glare.

Laurel was so embarrassed by her childish actions, she kept her eyes glued to her plate. She meticulously spooned every drop of the horrible pie into her mouth.

"Well, that was delicious," she said a few minutes later. "Everyone through?"

She tried to work her puckered mouth into a reasonable facsimile of a smile.

Both men immediately put down their forks and pushed their half-full pie plates back.

"Well, how about me helping you in the kitchen, Laurel," Dan offered.

"Gee, thanks, Dan. I'd appreciate that." They both began to gather up the empty plates.

Clay glanced up when Laurel accepted Dan's offer, his expression puzzled. "I'd be glad to help you, Laurel."

That Dan had his nerve! After all, Laurel was his date for the evening. Why she had tried to stomp him to death a few minutes ago he had no idea, but she was still *his* date!

"Oh, no, Clay. You and Cecile go into the living room, and Dan and I will clean up. We won't be long." Laurel assured him.

"Come on, Clay. Let's take a walk," Cecile urged. "The moon is beautiful out there tonight." She hooked her arm through Clay's and smiled up at him beguilingly.

Clay looked at Laurel, confusion clouding the blue of his eyes. "Are you sure you don't want me to help you?"

She smiled. "Positive. I know you and Cecile

want to get reacquainted. Dan and I will have things cleared away in no time at all."

She couldn't help but note the look of disappointment on his face as he limped painfully out of the room.

"Something wrong with your leg, Clay?" Laurel heard Cecile ask as they disappeared out the back door.

Laurel stacked the dishes in the dishwasher as Dan carried them in from the dining room. They made small talk as they worked, discussing business and the fact that the farm was all hers now.

Soon the conversation got around to the subject that had been on their minds daily: the continuing loss of turkeys and now the new fear that they would suffer a considerable loss of the new poults to cholera.

"I don't think that's what it is," Dan assured her, as he wiped the pots and pans dry. "The poults were all vaccinated at seven weeks, and they're taking the proper medication and vitamins in their water."

"It's been so hot and they've been overcrowding," Laurel fretted. "Last week the electric company was cutting limbs off the power wires, and the noise sent them into a dither."

"Well, you know as well as I do, a turkey is very easy to upset. I went up there the other night, and one of the heifers was standing next to number-three house making some noise. All the turkeys had moved to the rear of the building and were piling on top of each other. I thought for sure we were going to take a big loss due to suffocation, but thank goodness only a few died."

"Who keeps letting those cows out of their pasture! They shouldn't be grazing anywhere near the grow-out houses. That's why I spent all that money on new fences last year."

"I don't know. I wish I did," Dan said quietly. "But if we can hold out another month, we'll be able to get this batch of toms to the market with a fairly good profit, providing nothing else happens."

"We can't keep taking these losses, Dan. I'm afraid the farm will fold if these accidents keep happening."

Dan paused and leaned against the counter to peer at her with a playful frown. "Don't worry so much, Laurel. It'll make you old before your time." He reached out and affectionately tucked a lock of stray hair behind her ear. "You know I'll be here as long as you need me."

Laurel smiled her apology. "I know, and I don't know what I would do without you."

Once again she wished she could fall in love with Dan. Although he was ten years older than she, age had only enhanced his rugged good looks. At forty-one he had just the slightest touch of gray in his dark brown hair, and the light in his hazel eyes always twinkled no matter how bad things were. His pleasant nature always cheered her, and she realized how easy it would make things if she could only think of him in a more romantic way.

They had worked well together for the last five years. And since the farm was now hers, it would seem only natural to marry Dan and continue raising turkeys . . . but darn it! That wasn't what she wanted.

The time had come for her to live her own life without any commitments to anyone else for a while.

She realized that sounded very selfish, and maybe it was. But for once she wanted to have the freedom to pursue her music without any other deterrents.

Dan's finger drifted tenderly down the delicate curve of Laurel's face. "You know I would ask for so much more if you'd let me," he said softly.

Laurel's eyes dropped from his self-consciously. Dan didn't often speak of his feelings for her, but when he did, it was disconcerting.

"Oh, Dan. You're such a nice guy. I wish you could find someone who deserves your attentions."

Deep laughter rumbled somewhere within his broad chest as he realized that he was making her uncomfortable. Mercifully he broke the tension. "Yeah? Well, I've been hoping I could find someone too."

"Joy's been dead how long now?" Laurel asked gently.

"Over five years."

It was Laurel's hand that reached out now to offer quiet comfort to a very special friend. "I think some lucky girl is just waiting in the shadows for you, Dan Colburn."

"I wish that girl were you," he revealed quite candidly. "But I gave up hope a long time ago."

"I wish she were, too, but I have so many things I want to do with my life right now. . . ." Her voice trailed off painfully.

"All right. I can take a hint," he teased. "But you can't blame a man for trying."

A few minutes later they switched off the kitchen lights and walked out to the back porch.

"I was surprised to see Clay and Cecile together," Dan observed, as they started walking.

It was the custom for one of them to check the turkeys first thing every morning and last thing every night, and so they followed the path toward the brooder house.

"I asked Clay over tonight," Laurel confessed. "I always suspected that he had a crush on Cecile during school, and I thought it might be nice to get them reacquainted."

Laurel's eyes drifted to the couple sitting in the old porch swing, and a funny tug of something close to yearning yanked at Laurel's heartstrings.

Now, why would she resent Cecile sitting in the swing with Clay Kerwin?"

"Your sister's changed a lot since I last saw her," Dan commented.

"Yes, she has. She's finally grown up," Laurel admitted. "The past two years have taken their toll on her. She's had some pretty tough knocks."

"One thing about her hasn't changed. She's still as pretty as she ever was."

When Clay and Cecile noticed Dan and Laurel,

they promptly rose from the swing and walked over to join them.

"Where're you two going?" Cecile asked.

"Just out to check the turkeys.. Want to come along?" Laurel invited.

"Sure. You want to see the turkeys, Clay?"

Cecile looked up at Clay expectantly.

Laurel had to smother a laugh. She was sure that Clay had no burning desire to see the turkeys. Strangle a few thousand of them, maybe. Tear their feathers off one by one, maybe. But never just look at them!

"Sure, I'll come along with you," he agreed easily, casting a somewhat resentful glance in Laurel's direction. It had finally dawned on him what a fool he was.

Laurel hadn't invited *him* to dinner.

She had invited him to have dinner with Cecile!

As the two couples walked toward the brooder house Laurel couldn't help thinking how much she loved her home and how she would miss it when it was sold.

The farmhouse sat back in the shelter of several large oak trees, shielded from the harsh sun in the summer and the cold winds that blew in the winter. Although it was very old, the house had been remodeled several times and now had all the modern conveniences that a new one would have.

The farm was on forty acres of fertile land with a spring-fed creek and a large pond on the property. Besides the turkeys, Sam Henderson had run several head of cattle and a few horses on his pasture land.

For Clay's benefit, Laurel began to explain some of the procedures of turkey farming. Clay had visited the farm several times, but he actually knew very little about the operation itself.

"You'll notice the farm has four buildings, four hundred by fifty feet in size. The building on the left is the 'brooder house' where the young turkeys—or poults—are kept until they are six weeks old.

"The other three buildings on the right are 'grow-out' houses where the turkeys are placed to finish their growing period.

"The entire process takes about eighteen weeks and three days if we're raising toms, a little less for hens, before a turkey is ready for market."

Clay's eyes followed her hands as she pointed out each building. "Those large bins standing beside each building are the feeders," she informed him. "And the large building in the middle holds the central water supply and other equipment the farm needs to operate," Laurel continued.

"Then you raise around three broods of turkeys a year?" Clay asked.

"That's what we shoot for," Dan replied. "Of course, we're independent growers, and it depends on what the cash flow is, but we usually meet our goal."

"We're not going to this year," Laurel predicted glumly.

The moonlight drenched the path as the four approached the far building on the left. They quietly stepped inside.

"Watch your step, Clay," Cecile warned with a giggle.

The brooder house was not at all what Clay expected. It was immaculately clean and except for the strong smell of ammonia, it wasn't at all unpleasant.

"We check the houses about four times a day," Dan continued as they stood gazing on the peaceful poults. "We want to be sure the turkeys are doing okay."

"I think they're so cute," Cecile crooned, reaching down to pick up one of the sleeping babies. "Did you know that Laurel and Dan have to hand-feed the babies for the first six days?" she asked Clay.

"That must be a heck of a job," Clay commented, taking note of the thousands of turkeys filling the house.

"Oh, we put them in rings." Laurel pointed to round, aluminum cylinders stacked in the corner. "About six hundred babies to a ring. Then we take away the rings and put out several feeders. Each day we remove one, and at the end of six days they convert to the long string of feeders you see here before you.

"Their water supply is in the round feeders suspended from the ceiling throughout the building."

Clay perused the troughlike metal feeders running the length of the house and the turkeys' water supply hanging from the ceiling.

"We start the babies out by keeping the brooder house at around a hundred degrees, then drop the temperature five degrees a week. By the fourth week they won't need any heat at all," Dan supplied. He picked up a turkey and handed it to Clay. "As you can see, they provide their own heat."

Clay was amazed at the amount of heat emanating from the poult.

"How many have you got in here right now?" Cecile wondered as she affectionately stroked the baby turkey she held in her hand.

"These are toms, so we have around twenty-one thousand in here at the moment," Dan said with a tiny grin. "I think you might like turkey farming, Cecile."

"Well, I didn't used to, but I've changed my way of thinking about a lot of things lately." She smiled at him shyly and placed the poult back on the floor.

"Listen, I'm going to take a quick walk the length of the building," Dan said. "I'll be back in a minute."

He started off through the flock as Laurel finished explaining the brooder house operation to Clay.

She noticed that Cecile was listening more attentively than she used to when Laurel explained the operation to someone new.

When Dan returned, he smiled and assured Laurel that everything checked out. They left the baby turkeys resting peacefully.

When they came back to the house they had a second cup of coffee and sat around the old wooden table in the dining room chatting comfortably.

Around ten Clay and Dan noted the lateness of the hour and decided they had to be running along. Cecile and Laurel walked with them to the front door and bid them good night.

"You know, Clay is really nice," Cecile commented after the men had gone. "And so is Dan. I can't imagine why neither one of them hasn't married before now."

"You knew Dan lost his first wife?" Laurel asked.

Cecile looked thoughtful for a moment. "Oh, yes. I had forgotten. Well, anyway, I enjoyed Clay's company this evening."

"Maybe the reason he hasn't married is that he's been waiting for someone special," Laurel teased.

"Well, let's hope after tonight that he's getting closer to finding her." Cecile grinned impishly and ran up the stairway to her bedroom.

Laurel sighed and turned out the porch light. She heard a car door opening outside in the drive.

Clay Kerwin.

When had he turned into such a hunk?

Strolling into the darkened living room, Laurel sat down at the piano and began to play softly. Only the moonlight streaming through the open window illuminated the ivory keys.

The sweet, lilting tones of Mozart drifted peacefully out the window as Clay paused with his hand on the car door.

The sound of her music brought back painful memories of all the years he had been in love with her.

61

When he was younger, he used to sneak over to her house and sit under that very window and listen to her play for hours. He used to dream of the day when he would grow older and ask her to marry him.

Well, he had grown older.

He was thirty-three years old, and she still wasn't even close to being his.

There were dreams and then there were realities. And he was old enough to start facing up to some of those realities.

Clay Kerwin and Laurel Henderson.

A foolish dream that would never be reality.

He would catch the people responsible for terrorizing her farm, and he would wring their scrawny, no-good necks. Then she could sell the damn turkey farm and go on with her music, and he would be rid of her and her turkey feathers. That would be best for all concerned.

Besides, he consoled himself, she had to be the *worst* pie baker in the entire county!

Jerking the car door shut angrily, he sped down the drive in a cloud of dust, leaving the refrains of Mozart drifting tranquilly through the quiet night.

CHAPTER FOUR

Where do I go from here?

That nagging thought had skittered devilishly around in Laurel's mind all night long.

The farm and all its problems were entirely hers now, and she suddenly resented Samuel Henderson for leaving her alone with that responsibility.

Why? Why had her father cut Cecile out of his will and left Laurel to face the enormous burden of getting the farm back on its feet? Why had he left her to decide whether she should sell the land or not?

And what about Cecile?

Wasn't it possible that deep beneath that cool veneer of indifference she resented Laurel's total inheritance of what rightly should have been half hers?

That would seem only natural.

Even though Samuel Henderson and his oldest daughter had had their disputes, Cecile had to feel bitter toward her father for so coldly casting her aside, even in death.

Laurel sighed wistfully. How much easier it

would have been for Cecile to share in the monumental decisions than for Laurel to have to face them alone.

Laurel rose from the breakfast table and went to pour herself another cup of coffee.

The sun was just topping the small rise on the eastern horizon, spreading its hot rays over the parched land.

What they needed was a good rain, Laurel thought longingly. A good, drenching downpour that would soak the ground and cool the air temperature down to bearable.

Dan should be stopping by soon, she thought. Each morning after he checked the turkey houses he would stop in and share a few minutes over a cup of coffee with Laurel. They would discuss any new problems of the day and mull over the possible solutions.

Laurel smiled as she thought of how much Dan loved this farm.

He had come to the Hendersons looking for a job a little over five years ago. His wife had died while giving birth to a stillborn son. Laurel would never forget the look of desolation on Dan's rugged features as he stood before her father and asked for a job that day.

Perhaps "pleaded" would have been more of an appropriate word, for Dan Colburn was a desperate man. His very reason for living had suddenly been taken from him, and he was floundering in a sea of pain.

Although the last thing the farm needed was another person on the payroll, Sam's heart had gone out to the man, and he hired Dan on the spot.

For the first year Dan had had a hard time adjusting. But slowly he'd started to come back to life, and soon he was as much involved in running the farm as the Hendersons were.

At times pride would be so evident in Dan's eyes as they sent another flock of thriving turkeys to be processed that it was hard to distinguish who actually owned the farm, Sam Henderson or Dan Colburn.

The sound of a car pulling into the drive brought Laurel out of her reverie. She hurried over to the window, parting the crisply starched curtains and peering out the window.

Clay Kerwin was just getting out of his patrol car as she dropped the curtain back in place and rushed over to the mirror hanging beside the coatrack.

Checking her hair quickly, she licked her lips and wished she had put on a little more makeup that morning.

A sharp rap on the back screen interrupted her preening and sent her scurrying to open the back door.

The tall, imposing figure of the county sheriff filled the doorway as she let the door swing open. She smiled a pleasant good morning to his stern countenance.

"Hi, Clay!" she greeted brightly.

"Good morning, Laurel." He nodded crisply. He had an air of authority about him that made him look tough, lean, and definitely out of sorts this morning. "Hope I'm not out here too early, but I wanted to talk to you for a few minutes before I go on duty."

"Oh, I've been up for an hour," she assured him as she motioned for him to come in. "Going to be another hot one, isn't it?"

"Feels like it," he agreed, slipping his hat off politely as he stepped into the spotless kitchen.

"Have a seat and I'll get you a cup of coffee," she invited. "I'm afraid Cecile won't be up for a few hours yet if you came to see her."

"No coffee, thanks," he refused courteously. "And it isn't Cecile I've come to see. I wanted to talk to you."

Laurel looked at him in surprise. "Oh? You wanted to talk to me?"

Clay's eyes dropped self-consciously from hers and fastened on a fly buzzing around the kitchen screen.

"Yeah . . . for a few minutes, if you can spare the time."

"I can spare the time," she said, wondering what in the world Clay would want to see her about. "Want to go in the living room and sit down?"

"No, . . . no, this won't take a minute," he promised.

"Well, then, let's at least sit down at the kitchen table. You can watch me drink my cup of coffee."

They moved toward the massive round table and took their seats. Clay dropped his hat on the table and continued to avoid her inquisitive gaze as she waited for him to say something.

When he seemed to be having a hard time finding the right words to open the conversation, Laurel took pity.

"So, what have you been doing?"

Clay glanced up self-consciously. "Since when?"

"Since . . . high school," she filled in congenially.

"Since high school?"

"Yeah, what have you been doing with yourself since then?" she said, struggling and hoping to start the conversation rolling.

"Well, when I was seventeen, I—"

"No, not that far back," she said, stopping him abruptly.

Good heavens! She didn't have time to listen to the last sixteen *years* of his life.

"I meant, what have you been doing lately? Doesn't seem like I see you around much anymore," she clarified.

"I wasn't aware that you had been looking for me," he returned dryly, "but I've been busy with my job."

"Well, everyone says you're one of the best sheriffs our county's ever had."

He hadn't been worth a plug nickel so far in taking care of her problems, but that didn't mean he hadn't done a whole lot of good for the community otherwise.

"Thanks. I've been giving it my best," he acknowledged with a shy smile.

They sat for a few moments in strained silence.

"Sure you don't want a cup of coffee?" she offered again.

"No, thanks. I just had breakfast at the Kitchen Cupboard before I drove out."

"Breakfast at the Kitchen Cupboard, Laurel thought with irritation. That flashy Beatrice Mosely worked there, and rumor had it that Clay had been seen in her company at various times.

"Beatrice still work there?" she asked, fishing pleasantly.

"Yeah, she still works there."

"You eat there often?"

"Almost every morning. I don't do much cooking for myself," he admitted.

"Bea there every morning?"

Clay glanced at her suspiciously. "Yeah. Why?"

Laurel shrugged. "Just making conversation." She took a cautious sip of her hot coffee. "Must have awfully good food down there to keep you going back every morning," she pressed. Though, for the life of her, she didn't know why it mattered where he ate his breakfast every day.

"Real good. Bea knows the way to a man's heart."

The look of ill-concealed disgust that unexpectedly cropped up on Laurel's face caused him to backtrack hurriedly.

"Uh, she makes good biscuits," he said, correcting himself.

"I'll bet."

Clay's dark eyes locked with hers in a silent challenge. "Does it bother you where I eat my biscuits every morning?"

"Me?" She laughed airily. "Not at all, but it might bother Cecile when she finds out."

"Cecile? Why in the hell would it bother Cecile?" he asked incredulously.

"Well, because it probably just will," she said lamely. "After all, she's back now, and if you ever hope to attract her attention, you may have to give up eating breakfast at the Kitchen Cupboard every morning," she reasoned, forgetting for the moment that Clay had never actually said he was interested in her sister.

He shot her a look of disbelief. "If I want to attract her attention! Where did you get a harebrained idea like that?"

Laurel looked defensive. "From you."

Clay's face went blank. "When did I tell you I was interested in your sister? I don't recall us ever discussing anything more personal than the weather in the last few years."

"Oh, it wasn't lately," she said, feeling more and more puzzled. Why wouldn't he jump at the opportunity to bring all his old, pent-up feelings for Cecile out in the open? "It was back when we were all still in high school."

"In high school!"

"Ssshh!" Laurel cast a wary eye in the direction of the door. "You'll wake Cecile."

"Good. Maybe she'll hustle down here and tell me what in the world her crazy sister's talking about," he shot back in an irritable whisper.

"That won't be necessary," Laurel replied coolly. "I'm perfectly capable of explaining my statement. If you'll stop and think back for a moment to when we were in school, I'm sure you'll be able to answer your own question."

"I'm thinking," he pleaded, "but I don't have the slightest idea what you're talking about."

"Now think harder, Clay," she coaxed patiently. "Remember all the times you used to hang around Cecile when we were growing up? Remember all the hours you used to spend at the drugstore with the two of us after school? I remember that nearly every weekend you could find the three of us looking for something to do . . . oh, not together particularly, but it seemed like *you* were the one who always ended up getting stuck with the Henderson sisters if we couldn't find anyone else to cart us around that day."

"I remember one day when you and I spent the whole afternoon fishing, and Cecile took a nap on an old army blanket you had spread out on the grass," he granted hesitantly, hating to let her know that he hadn't forgotten one hour they had spent together in their youth.

Laurel's laughter filled the kitchen as she fondly recalled that same afternoon. Clay had patiently baited her hook with worms while Cecile slumbered peacefully nearby. After a couple of fishless hours they had grown tired of waiting for Cecile to wake up, so they mischievously tied assorted bobs and sinkers on her feet and hands. Then they'd snuck off behind some bushes to await her reaction when she woke to find the paraphernalia adorning her.

Laurel could still hear her sister's screams of indignation ringing across the quiet hillsides.

Both Clay and Laurel laughed now.

"You do remember," she accused.

Clay's face suddenly sobered. "Sure, I remember that day. I also remember that I gave you your first kiss that afternoon."

A soft blush covered Laurel's features as she dropped her eyes shyly away from his.

"Yeah, I do too. Naturally I had been pecked on the cheek by other boys, but you were the one who gave me my first real kiss."

Clay grinned boyishly. "I gather I've been superseded since then."

"Oh, certainly," she teased flippantly. "There's been a whole string of men to take your place since then."

"Really?"

For a moment Laurel was surprised at the serious tone Clay's voice had taken on.

"No, silly. Not really. I've been too busy running the farm to have very much of a love life."

"That's a shame," he noted, but Laurel detected an insincere twinkle in his eye.

"I'm sure you've kissed your fair share of women since then," she pointed out.

"Maybe so, but none of them were as pretty as you are."

"Why, Clay! Thank you. That's very nice of you to say," she said, accepting his compliment with a demure nod of her head. "But enough of this nonsense and back to the original topic of discussion."

"Which was?"

"How you've always had a secret crush on Cecile."

"Wrong."

"Wrong?" Laurel looked at him skeptically.

"That's right. I didn't have a crush on Cecile, I had one on you," he stated solemnly.

"Me?" His lips were moving, but she was positive she wasn't hearing him correctly.

"Why do you find that so hard to believe?"

"It was *me* you had the crush on?" she asked again.

When Cecile told her that she thought Laurel was the one Clay had been attracted to, the idea had seemed ridiculous. Now Clay was actually sitting here before her and verifying that very speculation. She was not only astonished, she couldn't think of one sensible thing to say in return.

"Well . . . uh . . . I always sort of assumed it was Cecile you were interested in," she stammered.

"No. It was you," he confirmed gravely.

"Oh?" She nervously wadded up the paper napkin she had been toying with. "Isn't that funny. I never even suspected."

"Yeah, hilarious." His dark brown eyes finally met hers. "So, from now on, how about letting me take care of getting my own women."

"You didn't enjoy being with Cecile last night?"

"Of course, I enjoyed being with her. She's a lovely woman, but it just so happens I like to choose my own dates if you don't mind."

"I don't mind," Laurel said hurriedly. "I really thought I was doing you a favor, Clay ... and Cecile was tickled pink when she found out you were coming to dinner." She paused and looked at him suspiciously. "Why didn't you tell me you didn't want to be Cecile's date last night?"

"I didn't know I was going to be with Cecile," he stated simply.

"You didn't? Well, who did you think I was asking you to be with ..." Her voice trailed off as the truth finally dawned on her. "Oh, my. Did you think I was asking you?"

Clay's smile was devoid of humor. "Pretty stupid, huh?"

"No, not stupid, but you should know me well enough to realize that I don't go around asking men to go out with me," she said curtly. He must have thought she had some nerve.

"I did find it a little hard to believe," he admitted.

"Well, I'm certainly sorry you misunderstood," she said, trying to hide her embarrassment.

"Don't worry about it. I just wanted to warn you to stay out of my personal business," he said rather brusquely, and got up from the table. "Cecile and I may see each other from time to time, but I don't want you attaching any significance to our dates."

"You may rest assured, I couldn't care less about your personal taste in women," she returned in a frosty tone, rising to follow him to the back door.

He certainly didn't need her to tell him that, he thought resentfully.

"Although," she continued, "if you ask my opinion, you would be a lot better off seeing my sister on a permanent basis than spending the taxpayer's time *and* money down at the Kitchen Cupboard eating Beatrice Mosley's moldy old biscuits!"

"You may be right," he agreed pleasantly, "but in the first place I don't recall asking you for your opinion. Secondly, Bea's biscuits are not moldy, and last but certainly not least, I don't plan on seeing *any* woman on a permanent basis. Is that clear?"

Laurel's face turned sullen. "Perfectly."

"Good. I'm glad we're on the same wavelength." He snapped his hat back on his head and opened the back screen. "Oh, yeah. One more thing."

"Yes?" She lifted her brow coolly.

"Why in hell did you keep kicking me under the table last night?"

She blushed. "Oh, I . . . it's a long story, and I'm sure you don't have time to hear it this morning."

"My shin is black and blue. I hope you know that."

"I said I was sorry!"

He snorted and opened the screen door.

"I don't suppose you've figured out how to take your turkeys to market without bringing them right through the public square, have you?"

"No, I haven't. And to be quite honest, Sheriff,

74

I have no intentions of changing my routine one iota." She smiled at him sourly.

"You keep stringing those feathers all over town, and I swear, Laurel, I'll be right there to write you a handful of littering tickets the next time you take a batch of turkeys to market."

He gave her a smile as sour as her own and let the screen door slam in her face as he left.

"And making faces at an officer of the law is going to get your rear in hot water one of these days," he tossed crossly over his shoulder as he strode out to his patrol car.

Laurel quickly sucked her tongue back in her mouth and frowned.

That man had eyes in the back of his head!

Dan stepped up on the porch as Laurel watched Clay pull out of the drive. Had a crush on her, my foot! she fumed. Well, if he did, he had certainly managed to get over it in a hurry.

"Did Clay have any news this morning?" Dan asked as she turned and started back into the house.

"No, he'd have to do something before he could come up with any news," she said sarcastically.

Dan laughed. "Doesn't sound like you're in too good a mood this morning."

"I'm sorry, Dan." Laurel smiled and began to simmer down. "Sit down and I'll get your coffee."

Dan took his seat at the table, and within a few minutes Laurel's disposition was back to normal. It was a relief to hear that there had been no new acts of vandalism on the farm during the night, and Dan and Laurel had an amiable visit.

Dan was just starting back to work when the sound of another car pulling up in the drive caught their attention.

"Now, who in the world could that be this early?" Laurel murmured. At this rate she would never get her work done today.

Paige Moyers stepped up on the back porch and knocked timidly at the door.

"Paige," Laurel said, greeting him affectionately as she opened the back door once more and admitted the newest visitor. "What brings you out here so early?"

"Thought I'd stop by on my way to the office," he explained as he bestowed a fatherly kiss on her cheek. "Hope it's not too early. Mornin', Dan."

"Good morning, Paige. I hate to rush off, but I have a bundle of work waiting for me out there," Dan apologized as he picked up his hat and headed for the door.

"Don't let me keep you." Paige waved him off with a chuckle. "Fine man, that Dan. Make someone a nice husband," the lawyer observed none too discreetly.

Laurel groaned inwardly. "Yeah, he sure would."

"As I said before I hope I'm not bothering you by coming out here this early," he reiterated. "But I had a few papers that need your signature this morning."

"Not, not at all. Coffee?"

"Don't mind if I do." Paige seated himself at the table comfortably and placed his briefcase before him.

Thirty minutes later their business was finished, and Paige was on his second leisurely cup of coffee.

"Don't suppose you've come to any decision yet on what you're going to do with the farm?" he prompted.

"No, I'm afraid not. I thought about it all last night, but it's probably going to take me a while to make up my mind."

Paige reached over and lay his large hand on top of her small one. "You wouldn't think I was stickin' my nose in where I shouldn't if I tried to give you some friendly advice, would you?"

"Oh, Paige. You know I always welcome your opinions. Why, you're just like family to me and always have been."

"I know, but I don't want to see you make any decision that's going to go against you in the long run. Sam would want me to make sure you were happy and doin' what's best for you."

Laurel let out a discouraged sigh. "I wish I knew what was best for me."

"Well, now. It's up to you and me to figure that out." He smiled.

"I don't know where to begin. I know that I would like to go on with my music, but I feel my loyalty should be here, at least until I can get things running smoothly again. It would be a shame to sell the farm under pressure, especially when Dan and I have worked so hard to get it where it is today."

"But don't you think the time has come for you to look out for your own happiness?" Paige prodded gently.

"That's just it, Paige. Where is my happiness? It isn't that I've been unhappy here, because I really haven't. After all, this is my home. And I have to think about Cecile. With Dad leaving her out of the will she really has nowhere to go right now. She has no formal training for any job other than being an actress, and you know how that turned out."

"You can't be responsible for Cecile all her life," Paige reasoned. "She's a grown woman, and one of these days she's going to have to learn to stand on her own two feet."

"She will. There's just been too many upsets in her life right now, and I don't want to cause her any more pain. What sort of person would I be to put her out of house and home and flaunt my inheritance in her face." Laurel sighed again. "Selling the farm right now just isn't practical."

"You were always too soft," Paige scolded. "Always thinking of the other person and letting life slide right on by you. How old are you now?"

"Thirty-one," she replied glumly.

"Thirty-one. Almost half your life over, Laurel, and what have you got to show for it?"

Nothing but a stack of bills and a flock of turkeys, she thought miserably.

"Well, I can see you still have a lot of thinkin'

to do," Paige confessed, closing up his briefcase. "I've got to be gettin' back to the office."

Laurel walked with Paige out to the porch. They both stood watching the sun work its way higher over the hilltop.

"I can see why you'd hate to part with this land," Paige sympathized as he drew in a deep breath of early-morning air. "It's so beautiful out here." He paused and looked at her expectantly. "Did you know that at one time my grandparents owned this land along with another hundred acres that lie just to the south of here?"

"No, I didn't realize that," Laurel confessed.

"Yes. I can remember Grandma Moyers tellin' about how her and Grandpa used to work this land from sunup to sundown, trying to scratch out a livin' for their family. The truth is, I guess Grandpa did work himself to death because he died before I was ever born. Those were hard times."

"I'm sure they were," Laurel agreed sympathetically.

Paige's eyes moved slowly over the land, taking in its gentle hills and valleys. "Yes. Those were hard times for everyone," he said reminiscently. "Grandpa and Grandma worked hard and never had a thing to show for it when they died. That's sad, you know. A man workin' his whole life and never havin' a thing to show for it when he dies."

Paige seemed to drift off into the past, leaving Laurel for a moment.

Suddenly he snapped out of his wanderings

and returned to the present. "Maybe you should sell the land to me," he suggested. "I'd kind of like to have it back in the family . . . you know, as sort of a testimony that Grandpa and Grandma didn't work all their life for nothing."

"Oh, I don't know, Paige. I'll just have to think about it," Laurel said gently.

"I'll pay top dollar for it," he tempted.

"We'll see."

"Well, at least promise me that if you do decide to sell, you'll let me know first. This land has a lot of sentimental value to me, and I would never forgive myself if I let it fall into anyone else's hands."

"Now that I can do," she said, smiling. "You will be the first one who has a shot at buying this farm if I decide to sell."

As Paige pulled out of the drive Laurel walked back in the house, mulling over their conversation.

Paige was serious about wanting to buy the land.

When he mentioned it in his office the other day, she had thought it was just in passing, but apparently the land did mean something to him.

Well, it would certainly be easy to sell to an old friend like Paige. At least the land would still be in the family . . . sort of.

Maybe she would give his offer some serious thought. But for now, the morning was slipping by and she hadn't accomplished a thing.

Her mind skipped back to Clay Kerwin.

He had had a crush on *her* in high school. Could you beat that!

Shrugging her shoulders, she went into the kitchen. She started pulling out flour and sugar from the cabinet. Since she had wasted so much time this morning, anyway, it wouldn't hurt to bake something fresh before she got all busy with the turkeys.

The unbidden thought entered her head. Gooseberry bread.

She still had gooseberries left, and that sounded rather unusual and tasty. And if it turned out well, which she seriously doubted, perhaps she might take an extra loaf by Mr. Know-It-All Kerwin's office.

She would show him *she* could bake a decent loaf of bread.

It would be a small, very discreet, peace offering on her part for misleading him last night.

Maybe he would accept her offering and maybe he wouldn't.

Either way it didn't matter.

She would have done her part, and her conscience would be clear even if his wasn't.

CHAPTER FIVE

The gooseberry bread was cooling on the kitchen cabinet a little before noon, its fresh-baked fragrance filling the house.

Since there was no pressing business that day, Laurel had decided to take the entire morning off, a treat she rarely allowed herself.

By noon, however, the heat of the day was mounting steadily, and Laurel decided to check the brooder house to see how the poults were doing. There were large fans in the turkey houses, and later on in the afternoon they would be turned on to help keep the turkeys cooler.

After a hurried shower she slipped on a pair of shorts and a lightweight T-shirt, then ran a brush through her thick mass of auburn hair.

For a moment she debated on whether to pull it back in a ponytail. It would be much cooler, but she hated the way it made her look thirteen years old.

All of a sudden Laurel's attention was diverted to a loud commotion coming from the direction of one of the grow-out houses.

Her brush clattered on the vanity as she

whirled and ran out of the room, bounding down the stairs two at a time.

She rushed by Cecile, who was hurrying down the stairway herself to see what all the uproar was about.

Both women were out the back door and running toward the turkeys in number-three house as Dan passed them in a dead run.

"What's going on?" Laurel shouted.

"Damned if I know!" Dan hollered back. "Something's got the turkeys in a panic!"

"They sound like they're about to croak!" Cecile exclaimed in short, gasping breaths as she tried to keep up with Dan and Laurel's flying feet.

"I can't imagine what's wrong," Laurel shot back, her face revealing her deep concern.

From the erratic sounds of the turkeys she knew she could be facing another major loss. They sounded as if they were piling on each other. Bruising at this late date would be sure to result in downgrading when she took the turkeys to market in a few weeks.

Laurel and Cecile reached the grow-out house moments after Dan. They rushed through the doorway.

The sight that met their eyes was one of total chaos.

Dan was trying to chase down a large shaggy dog that was barking at the top of his lungs and scattering the turkeys wildly in every direction.

The birds were bouncing off the walls and running into each other frantically. As Laurel had feared, they were piling. She knew that if she couldn't get them off each other, and quickly, several hundred would be suffocated in a matter of minutes.

At the sound of Dan's voice the dog stopped in his tracks. His large, furry tail began to wag sheepishly as he hunkered down on his front paws and watched wearily as Dan approached him in angry strides.

"Tramp! What in the devil are you doing in here?" Dan demanded impatiently.

He knelt down, took hold of the dog's collar, and proceeded to drag the mischievous canine out of the turkey house. Laurel started talking to the turkeys in an effort to calm them down.

They recognized her voice instantly but were so excited, it took over an hour for Dan, Laurel, and Cecile to get the flock to settle down once more.

The actual loss of turkeys was not as high as first feared, but the damages would be heavy in loss of yield per pound at the market.

"How did Tramp get in here, Dan?"

Laurel felt her temper rising as they walked the length of the grow house to be sure the turkeys had settled back to normal.

"I don't know how he got in here," Dan admitted.

Laurel paused and faced him, her cool gaze almost an open challenge. "You have to admit that it does seem strange that it was your dog, doesn't it?"

She knew she was going to say something she

would regret. Just because Dan's dog had been the culprit in this most recent mayhem didn't mean a thing. Anyone could have let the dog in the grow-out house. Laurel knew that, but the past few weeks had begun to take their toll on her. She was beginning to suspect even her closest friends of wrongdoing.

Dan stiffened. "I suppose. If a person chose to look at it that way." His steady gaze met hers directly. "Are you accusing me of turning my dog loose in this grow-out house?"

Was she? Laurel wondered.

Dan loved the farm as much as if it were his own. He would have no reason to see the business go under and Laurel be forced to sell . . . would he?

"Now, look, you two," Cecile interceded quickly when she saw that things were going to get out of hand. "Don't either one of you say something that you'll regret later. The crisis is over now and you're both still upset."

She stepped up and hooked her arm through Dan's. "Come on, Dan. Let's go back to the house and I'll fix you something cold to drink."

"No, I want to hear Laurel's answer." Dan refused to budge from his angry stance.

"And I'm sure she's dying to give it to you . . . but later." Cecile gave him one of her famous smiles that any man was helpless to refuse, and Dan allowed himself to be docilely led away from the scene of smoldering tension a few moments later.

Watching his tall form disappear toward the

house, Laurel was instantly ashamed of her outburst of totally unwarranted suspicion.

What in the world had gotten into her?

How could she have practically accused Dan of being her enemy? Good, dependable Dan, who had never done anything but try to help her since the first day he had come to work here.

Was she really so paranoid?

Unexpectedly her temper rose to the surface again.

Clay Kerwin was the one she should really take her anger out on! Where was he when all these accidents were happening?

She would bet her last dollar he wasn't out beating the bushes for the culprits responsible for this newest outrage.

Taking one last look around her, she cautiously began to make her way toward the exit of the building. The turkeys were calm now, and she wanted to keep them that way.

Laurel's clothes were sticking to her uncomfortably in the heat as she made her final rounds of each grow-out house. She decided to switch the large fans on a little earlier than usual.

As she finished with the brooder house, Dan's dog ran around the side of the building and yapped at her playfully.

"Go home, Tramp," she ordered in a grumpy tone.

Tramp wagged his tail happily, undisturbed by her less than hospitable greeting as he continued to circle her and yip sociably.

Again the question surfaced in her mind. Who had put Tramp in that grow-out house?

Certainly it was someone who knew the havoc it would cause. A great deal of money had been lost this afternoon due to this unfortunate incident, and Laurel was bound and determined to get to the bottom of all the trouble.

As the day wore on, Laurel's mood did not improve. On the contrary, it only worsened.

By late afternoon her temper had gotten the better part of her common sense, and she decided to personally inform a certain sheriff of this latest round of intimidation.

Besides, she had that stupid gooseberry bread she had baked for him that morning. She was too conservative to throw it away, and she wasn't about to eat it herself, so she might as well give it to him.

Dan had dropped by the house briefly that afternoon to tell her that he had called Clay's deputy, Buck, to report the incident of the dog in the grow-out house.

Laurel had bent over backward to be pleasant to her foreman, hoping he would forgive her for their heated encounter.

After being offered a glass of lemonade, which he promptly refused, he had stalked off the porch toward the barn without another word.

It seemed to Laurel that Dan was more hurt than mad, and that thought upset her even more.

All this because Clay Kerwin was not doing his job!

You shouldn't go talk to him, she kept warning herself as she showered and changed to go out. You'll only end up fighting again, and that won't help matters in the least.

Even as she got in the pickup and inserted the key in the ignition, she was still trying to talk herself out of what she was about to do.

You'll only make him hate you, she cautioned. Laurel paused to frown. A week ago she wouldn't have worried about what Clay thought of her.

Her frown deepened.

So why was she sitting here in her teal-blue sun dress, smelling like a rose garden, as mad as a wet hen but still on her way over to see him?

She hadn't the faintest idea.

With a resigned shrug she started the truck and pulled out of the drive. Although by now Clay would probably be off duty, she decided to stop by the jail first on the remote chance that he would be concerned enough about her problem to put in a little overtime.

There was neither hide nor hair of the county sheriff or his patrol car when she pulled up in front of his office.

Entering the sheriff's office, she found Buck Gordon reading a newspaper, his feet propped up on the desk.

Upon seeing her the deputy was instantly on his feet, a big friendly smile dominating his rugged features.

"Afternoon, Laurel."

"Afternoon, Buck." She looked around the office suspiciously. "Clay already gone home?"

"Yes, ma'am. Left a couple of hours ago." He stopped, and his eyes narrowed worriedly. "You haven't had any more trouble out your place, have you?"

"No, not since the dog this afternoon. You say he's been gone a couple of hours?"

"Yeah, 'bout that," Buck speculated. "Sure was sorry to hear about the ruckus with the dog—"

"Is he on official business?" Laurel interrupted. It was only five thirty now. That meant Clay had left the office around three thirty, at least an hour before he usually got off.

"No, he just knocked off early today." Buck grinned. "Was there something I could help you with?"

Knocked off early! What a waste of her tax dollars! It also shot down the theory that he was putting in any extra time on her problem.

"Do you have any idea where he went?"

"Well, now I don't rightly know . . ." Buck paused and scratched his head as he mulled over the question. "If I were guessin', I'd probably say he went on over to his place."

"Thanks, Buck." Laurel was gone before he could even say good-bye.

Sheriff Clay Kerwin lived about ten miles out on the outskirts of town in a rambling, old two-story house. The house sat on a hilltop overlooking most of his twenty acres.

As Laurel drove along the shaded lane to his home, she was reminded of how much the house and settings resembled her own. Maybe that was why she instinctively knew she was going to love the house, even before she had actually seen it.

As she pulled in the drive, two large basset hounds came sauntering over to greet her.

She couldn't help but laugh at the woebegone expression in each of their eyes as they gazed up at her, their tails thumping loudly on the ground.

"Hi, fellas," she greeted them as she leaned down and affectionately patted them both on the head.

As Laurel turned toward the house she noticed that there was another car sitting in front of Clay's patrol car.

It suddenly dawned on her that she was being awfully pushy by coming to his home to conduct business. She debated for a moment whether or not to turn around and go back home. Then she decided that since he had taken off early that afternoon, as a taxpayer she was entitled to these few minutes, even if he wasn't officially on duty.

Stepping quickly up to the front door, she pressed the door bell before she lost her nerve.

A bee droned lazily in one of the neatly clipped hedges that surrounded the porch.

There was no answer.

She pressed the door bell again.

A few moments passed and still no sound behind the door.

She pressed the door bell once more. He was here; she knew he was. His car was in the drive along with that other one.

Maybe he was trying to hide from her again.

That thought sent her finger back on the door bell persistently, determined to smoke him out of his hiding place.

When another five minutes passed and he still had not opened the door, her temper was boiling again.

That ratfink *was* hiding!

Stomping back off the porch, she headed back for her truck, cursing the Clay Kerwins of the world under her breath in a very unladylike manner.

Just as she started to open the truck door, the sound of a woman's laugh floating softly through the air caught her attention.

Laurel paused and listened intently as a man's laugh joined the woman's.

So, he was there.

Tiptoeing quietly around the side of the house, Laurel followed the sounds of gaiety coming from the backyard. She could hear splashing now and more laughter as she grew closer.

As she rounded the last corner she stopped and stared at the scene before her.

Beatrice Mosely, the "old biscuit maker" from the café, and Clay were swimming in a glistening, oval-shaped pool. And having quite a good time by the looks of things!

Beatrice was giggling as Clay tried to outrun her around the pool.

It was abundantly clear to Laurel that Beatrice's biscuits were not the only thing Clay Kerwin was interested in as he grabbed her foot and both of them went in the water in a flurry of splashes and laughter.

Laurel strolled casually over to the edge of the pool and sat down, waiting for them to resurface.

Seconds later they both came back to the top, gasping for breath.

"Clay Kerwin, you naughty old boy!" Beatrice giggled again and halfheartedly worked at readjusting her swimsuit top. "I do declare, I thought you were going to drown me for sure!"

Clay's deep laughter rumbled in his broad chest as he flipped his wet hair out of his face and wiped his eyes. "Who, me? Why, I wouldn't—" His voice broke off as he opened one eye.

Good grief. Laurel Henderson was sitting on the edge of the pool looking as if she could strangle him!

"Laurel, where in the hell did you come from?" he managed to choke out in a surprised voice.

Beatrice turned and glanced up at Laurel. "Well, I do declare. I didn't know we had company." She batted her long, fake eyelashes in Laurel's direction and smiled. "You must walk like a cat, honey."

Laurel smiled at her sourly.

Clay swam over to where Laurel was sitting and hoisted himself out of the water to sit beside her. Reaching for one of the navy-blue towels draped across a lawn chair, he toweled his hair partially dry, then wrapped the thick terry cloth around his neck.

Laurel tried to avoid letting her eyes rest on the bronzed, smooth skin of his broad chest.

Clay Kerwin had muscles on top of muscles!

"To what do I owe this pleasure?" he asked politely.

"I'm sorry to interrupt your ... party," she began, then stopped and licked her dry lips.

Gad! He was simply beautiful without any clothes on. All virile and bronzed and so darn sexy.

Willing her eyes to focus elsewhere, she tried to remember why she was here. "I ... think I wanted to talk to you."

She smiled weakly, painfully aware that she must look like a grinning imbecile.

"What do you think you wanted to talk to me about?" He cocked a dark brow inquisitively and grinned at her.

"Oh, darlin', are you getting out for a while?" Beatrice paddled over to where Laurel and Clay were sitting and smiled up prettily. "I'm gettin' lonesome in here all alone."

"Let's take a break, Bea," Clay suggested pleasantly. "I think Laurel needs to discuss some business with me."

"Okey-dokey."

Laurel and Clay's eyes followed Beatrice as she swam over to the ladder and pulled herself up.

Laurel's eyes widened; Clay's were discreetly noncommittal. Nevertheless, Laurel noted that his gaze was still glued on Bea's voluptuous figure as she climbed out of the water clad in the briefest bikini a man could ever hope to encounter. Only Bea's bare essentials were covered and then only just within the realm of decency.

Her slender frame glistened with suntan oil and dripping water as she sashayed over to Clay and unwrapped the towel from around his neck.

"Do you mind, Sheriff?"

The sheriff didn't mind—that was obvious—as he smiled and handed her the towel. "I believe you and Laurel Henderson have met?"

"Sure thing!" Bea flashed Laurel a friendly smile. "How are you, honey?"

"Fine. I'm sorry I've interrupted your swim," Laurel apologized guiltily. "I didn't realize the sheriff had company."

"Oh, we're happy to have you stop by," Bea assured her. "I'll just run in and make us all a cold drink. Iced tea be all right with everyone?"

Laurel nodded mutely.

She had no idea Clay and Bea were so . . . cozy. *We* are glad to have you stop by?

"You just relax and take care of your business," Bea called as she swayed off toward the house. "I'll be back in no time at all!"

When calm descended over the yard once more, Laurel took off her sandals and dipped her feet in the tepid water of the pool.

The sound of jar flies tuning up for the summer evening filled the air as Clay glanced over at Laurel. "Now, before you start climbing my back," he said quietly, "I want you to know I'm well aware of Dan's dog being in one of your grow-out houses today."

"And I see you've put in long, backbreaking hours to try to find out who put the dog there," Laurel returned coolly.

"I know you're not going to believe it, but I have," he defended.

"Yes, I know you have," she acknowledged with a curt smile. "I went by the office earlier, and Buck said you had left early today, so I immediately assumed you were out tracking down the criminals. Sure enough, you were over here working your little heart out. You must be exhausted."

Clay's clear blue eyes met hers sternly. "It just so happens that I left the office early today because it's my birthday. This is the first time I've left early since I took office."

"This isn't your birthday," she scoffed. "Your birthday is in the winter."

Clay looked at her smugly. "This is too my birthday," he challenged.

"Clay! I distinctly remember your birthday is somewhere around Christmas," she argued.

"Look. I ought to know when my own birthday is," he shot back. "And I say it's today!"

"Well, all right! Don't get so bent out of shape," she finally relented. "I must have been mistaken, but I could have sworn I went to your birthday party one time just before Christmas."

Clay paused and tried to recall the event. "That was probably my brother Sloan's birthday. He was born on the twentieth of December. I was born on the twenty-third of July. Okay?"

"That's fine with me," she returned sharply. "Let's change the subject."

"All right." He leaned back on his elbows and stared up in the sky. "It's been hot today."

"Yes, it has, but I didn't come all the way over here to talk about the weather, either," she grumbled.

Clay sighed and kicked water at her playfully. "Okay, what do you want to talk about, cranky?"

"I want to talk about what you're going to do about my problem."

"And I don't want to talk about *that* on my birthday," he reasoned. "We'll only end up in a quarrel, so let's talk about something else."

Laurel looked at him in exasperation. "What else is there to talk about?"

"Okay. Let's start with you and Dan," he suggested.

"Me and Dan?" That was the last topic of discussion she would have suggested. "What about us?"

"How involved are you with your foreman?" he asked bluntly.

Laurel instantly resented his question. "That's none of your business."

"Yes it is," he returned calmly.

"What makes you think so?"

"Because he might just be involved in all this trouble, Laurel," he pointed out quietly. "It was his dog in that grow-out house today, wasn't it?"

"Yes, but he didn't have anything to do with that," Laurel told him defensively, still feeling guilty for having had the same thoughts earlier today. "Dan loves that farm as much as I do."

"That's right, he does. He loves it so much, I don't think he could stand to see it leave your hands and go to someone else."

"What are you talking about?" she demanded irritably.

"Stop and think about it, Laurel. Dan knows you want to sell the farm eventually and go on with your music. Dan isn't a rich man, and if he could cause enough trouble to force you into selling the farm to him at a big loss, isn't it possible he might want to do that?"

"That's crazy."

"It may be," Clay allowed. "But it's also very possible."

"Dan Colburn is the nicest man I've ever met," she upheld. "Why, I think he even wants to marry—" She broke off suddenly before she gave away too many details of her personal life.

"Marry you? That doesn't surprise me. Are you sleeping with him?"

Laurel's eyes were cold as she turned to meet his studious gaze. "That is certainly none of your business!"

"Are you sleeping with him, Laurel?" he persisted sternly.

Shooting him a frosty glare, she thought about his question for a moment before answering. It was really none of his business, but just to keep the records straight, she decided to give him an honest answer.

"No."

"Why not? You're certainly old enough to have needs just like the rest of us."

That was true. She did have needs, but her life had been too busy to fulfill those needs.

She knew it was high time she ventured out into the sexual world, but she certainly wouldn't be happy stepping into a casual affair, and besides, there just weren't that many eligible men around this town.

"Because he doesn't appeal to me . . . that way." Her gaze drifted wistfully over to Clay's manly physique.

Now, if Dan looked like Clay, it would be a different story. Oh, Dan was nice-looking enough. But the sight of him had never sent her pulse racing like the sight of a nearly nude Clay was doing at the moment.

"Well, what sort of man does appeal to you?" he asked casually.

"I don't know," she hedged. "Let's talk about something else. Are you sleeping with Bea?"

His mouth dropped open. "What?"

"I said, are you sleeping with Bea? Apparently you want candidness, so I'm giving it to you."

He chuckled. "I think that's a little too candid."

"Why? You wanted to know if I'm sleeping with Dan."

"Only because it relates to the case. I don't want to see you get hurt if it turns out Dan is in on any of this."

"Oh, I see. Well, it doesn't matter, anyway. I know you're sleeping with her," she told him blithely.

"Is that right? And where do you get your information?"

"In a town this size you can hardly keep a thing like that a secret," she chided. "You might as well admit it."

"I'm not admitting anything." He flashed her a wicked grin. "If I were having the supreme pleasure of sleeping with you, would you want me to be spreading it all over town?"

Laurel thought about that for a moment.

Of course not. And she knew he wouldn't.

Clay would be the perfect kind of a gentlemen to have an affair with. He had always been closemouthed about his personal life, and the years hadn't changed that.

"No," she admitted honestly.

"There you go. Anyway, I didn't ask you who you were sleeping with," he reasoned. "I only wanted to know if Dan was included."

Laurel's gaze narrowed. "You make me sound like a heifer in heat!"

He reached over and tipped her face longingly. "Well, lady, if you are, save me a place in line."

Her heart lurched as she saw the complete sincerity in his gaze.

Was Clay Kerwin actually making a pass at her? If so, she was sorely tempted to take him up on it.

"Stop teasing me!" she demanded uneasily.

"Teasing? I've never been more serious in all my life." He paused for a moment. "But back to the original subject. I'm checking into Dan. Buck thinks it might be the Rowden boys causing your trouble."

"The Rowden boys? I hadn't thought of them," Laurel admitted.

Jake and Eddy Rowden lived about three miles down the road from her farm and had been in and out of trouble most of their lives. They were both in their early twenties and had never done a decent day's work. Why hadn't she thought of them earlier?

The sound of Bea opening the French doors to bring out their cold drinks prevented further conversation. Clay's hand dropped away from Laurel's chin.

The three drank their glasses of iced tea and shared small talk.

Half an hour later the gathering shadows reminded Laurel that she had stayed longer than necessary.

But for some reason she was reluctant to leave, even though she knew she was imposing on their date.

"I really must be going," she said at last. She set her empty glass on the tray and reached for her sandals.

"We're going to cook some steaks here in a minute," Clay protested. "Why don't you stick around and help celebrate my birthday with us?"

"Oh, I couldn't do that," she murmured, willing her heart to slow down from its erratic fluttering.

She was sure Bea would simply love that idea!

"I'd like for you to," he declared openly.

"No, I'd better be going." She stood up and put her sandals back on. "Thanks for the drink."

"Anytime, honey. It was nice seeing you," Bea said brightly.

"Wait a minute. I'll walk you around to your truck," Clay suggested.

"Don't be long, sweetie. I'm going to put the steaks on in a few minutes," Bea cautioned him.

"I'll only be a minute."

It was growing darker as Clay took Laurel's arm and escorted her around the house.

As he helped her in the truck she remembered the gooseberry bread she brought him. Reaching for the foil-wrapped package she extended it to him with a grin.

"Here, I almost forgot. Happy birthday."

The smile that lit his face was nothing less than radiant. "You *did* remember it was my birthday!"

Laurel didn't want to dash his newfound happiness. "I hope you like it."

"I will! What is it?" he asked enthusiastically.

"Gooseberry bread."

His smile was still intact, but Laurel sensed a feeling of disappointment steal over him.

"Oh, really. Great. My favorite . . . gooseberry bread."

Laurel started the truck, feeling extremely glad that she'd gone to all the trouble to bake the bread for him that morning.

"Hey, wait a minute," he called hurriedly. "Isn't it customary to give an old friend a birthday kiss?"

Laurel glanced at him uneasily. "I . . . suppose."

He leaned in closer to her. "Are you serious?"

"Are you?"

"You're darn right I'm serious."

"What do you think Bea would think about that?" Laurel teaseed.

"Bea doesn't have any hold on me."

"I don't care, it's still tacky to be kissing another girl out in the driveway while your date slaves over a hot grill cooking your dinner," she scolded with a twinkle in her eye.

Here she'd come over to bawl him out and had not only *not* bawled him out but was sitting here flirting with him like a teenager.

"You'll just have to collect that birthday kiss some other time."

Clay reluctantly withdrew his head from the car window. "Maybe you're right. But I may just hold you to that promise, Laurel Henderson."

She looked at him and gave him a saucy wink. "We'll see."

Suddenly his head popped back through the open window, and he swooped down and took her mouth in a brief, but very tantalizing, kiss.

Laurel was so shocked, she couldn't do anything but sit there and totally enjoy it.

"There. Think about that while I'm waiting to collect," he said with just a touch of smugness in his voice.

And as she drove away light-headed, she knew she probably wouldn't think of anything else for days.

CHAPTER SIX

Dawn's rosy rays were filtering through the bedroom windows when Laurel opened her eyes the next morning.

She stretched lazily and yawned.

It was going to be another hot one. The rain had still not materialized, and the days seemed to grow longer, drier, and hotter.

For a moment Laurel lay thinking back on what had taken place the night before.

Going over to Clay's had been foolish. Although he had handled it well, she was sure he must have been embarrassed when she showed up and interrupted his date. She frowned when thoughts of Beatrice Mosely intruded.

Gadzooks! Was she built!

Then her thoughts drifted to Clay. Gadzooks! Was he *ever* built!

A tiny smile crossed her lips as she yawned again and closed her eyes. Imagine. She was lying here thinking about Clay Kerwin in a romantic way.

All the years she had known him and not paid the least attention to him and all of a sudden he had her nearly panting in his wake.

It was almost impossible to keep from wondering what it would be like to have a man like Clay make love to her.

She wasn't at all experienced in the ways of love . . . at least not like the majority of women her age were. Oh, she had dated and had some pretty heavy petting sessions in her time. But as far as actually going to bed with a man—she never had.

A feeling of resentment slowly crept over her. Thirty-one years old and still inexperienced.

That was unnerving.

She supposed she ought to have an affair.

There was certainly no one around she wanted to marry, so the only logical solution would be to pick some nice man who lived in town and have an affair with him.

That way she would know what her friends were talking about when they said "the earth moved."

Yes, an affair was what she needed.

She would still have her freedom to do as she wished, but she would no longer be thirty-one years old and pure as the driven snow.

After all, hadn't her very own sister told her that was exactly what she needed to spice up her dreary existence? What were Cecile's exact words? "What you need is a good old blockbuster of a love affair with some dashing man who will make you forget all about the conservative side of Laurel Henderson."

Now, who would she have an affair with if she decided to ditch her scruples and actually proceed with this unexpected, but certainly titillating, brainstorm?

Well, there was always Dan.

Laurel frowned. No, that wouldn't be fair to him. He would end up wanting to marry her, and she didn't want that. She would have to choose someone who was impartial, didn't want a lasting relationship, and could keep his mouth shut. Rumors flew like wildfire in this small town. She would not want to give the town any more juicy tidbits to toss about than she had to.

There was Bill Nesbitt down at the pharmacy, but no ... not him. He was nearly bald and wasn't even thirty-five years old yet.

Brad Miller lost his wife last year, and she had heard he was pretty lonely. He might welcome a brief affair. No, she barely knew him, and anyway, he wasn't her type.

Wracking her brain to come up with another likely candidate, she finally had to admit that other than Clay Kerwin, there just wasn't any man in town she would seriously consider having an affair with.

Her meandering daydreams suddenly came to a screeching halt, and her eyes shot open.

Clay Kerwin. Now why did *he* pop up in her mind?

Well, it wasn't such an alarming thought. Clay was unattached, nice-looking, had a respectable job, and she certainly knew him well enough to feel comfortable with him . . . at least she would after the first initial shyness wore off.

He was every ounce a gentleman, and she was sure he had all the experience necessary to make a brief, completely detached love affair very rewarding.

On top of all of that he would keep his mouth shut.

That was extremely important in matters such as these.

So, she was now forced to give strong consideration to the local sheriff as a prospective contender for an admittedly preposterous idea.

And that's exactly what she did for the next couple of days.

The most important thing would be to talk him into having the affair in the first place.

She had no idea how receptive he would be to such a blatant proposal, and she had to admit that she didn't know the first thing about having an affair, but it was high time she learned! Should she approach him with her offer? Would he laugh in her face and tell her to get lost?

Laurel had still not decided what to do a week later as she stood in the kitchen drinking a glass of water before she went up to bed.

It was an unusually hot night, and every window in the house was thrown wide open to try to catch the slightest breeze. The air-conditioning unit was on the blink, and a service man wasn't able to come out until some time next week, so Cecile and Laurel had been suffering.

"I can't stand much more of this," Cecile said

as she entered the kitchen, wiping her neck with a wet washcloth.

"I know. It's miserable, isn't it?"

Laurel glanced at her sister. Cecile had a dress on instead of her usual attire of skimpy shorts and halter. "Are you going somewhere?"

"Yeah, I thought I might take a walk. You know, it's so hot and all," Cecile grumbled.

"Alone?"

"What do you mean by that?" her sister asked defensively.

Laurel was surprised by the sharp edge to Cecile's voice. "Why, nothing. It's getting late, and with all the trouble we've been having lately, I just thought it might not be safe for you to go wandering around by yourself at this hour."

"I'm a big girl now, perfectly capable of taking care of myself," she said curtly, and walked over to the back screen. "Don't wait up for me."

"Don't worry, I hadn't planned on it," Laurel muttered under her breath as the screen door slammed shut loudly.

What in the world was stuck in Cecile's craw?

Wandering through the house a few minutes later, she paused and sat down at the piano, playing for a few minutes and letting the music wash over her soothingly.

But the night was so muggy and warm, she couldn't sit still for very long, so she soon gave it up. Laurel continued her journey through the house switching off lights.

She had just turned the light off in the den when she happened to glance out the window into the barnyard. She paused in the darkness and watched as Cecile came from around the barn with her arm looped through a man's.

Laurel crept over to the window and lifted the curtain to peer out, trying to make out who in the world Cecile was with.

Her mouth dropped open as she recognized Dan Colburn's tall form in the bright moonlight.

What were Dan and Cecile doing out there together? He had gone home for the evening hours ago.

The sound of Cecile's soft laughter floated through the open window as Laurel let the curtain drop back in place. She stood mulling over the fact that her sister was taking a moonlight walk with Dan Colburn.

She wasn't aware that they had been seeing each other.

A dark seed of suspicion suddenly started to grow in her. Was it possible that Cecile was in cahoots with Dan? Were they responsible in some way for the vandalism that had taken place on the farm recently?

After all, Cecile had been cut out of the will, and no matter what she said, she would have to resent that.

No, that was utter nonsense!

Laurel shook the thought irritably out of her head.

Her trouble had started long before Cecile had come back home. She absolutely refused to sink so low as to start accusing her own flesh and blood of trying to run her out of business.

Cecile and Dan had probably run into each other tonight quite by accident. It wasn't that unusual for Dan to come back to the farm in the evening.

Determined to not let the incident upset her, she hurried upstairs to her bedroom and slammed the door loud enough to assure herself that she meant business.

But the nagging thought kept cropping up as she showered and got ready for bed. Laurel couldn't even concentrate on the book she was reading to help her fall asleep.

Cecile had still not come in the house yet. If she and Dan had met just by chance, then they were enjoying every minute of it, she thought crossly, switching off the light by her bed.

Sliding out of the bed, she walked over to the window and peered out into the moon-drenched barnyard.

No sign of the worrisome couple.

She stood for a moment looking out over the fields, lit almost as bright as day by yellow moonbeams.

Full moon, she thought wistfully.

Lover's moon.

A strange ache stole over her, and she wished she had someone to share that moon with.

From the corner of her eye she saw a figure suddenly dart from behind one of the old oak trees next to the brooder house and run the short distance to another tree thirty yards away.

She watched as the shadowy figure made its

way past each grow-out house and finally disappear behind the last one.

The culprit was getting ready to strike again!

Reaching for her thin housecoat, she rushed over to her dresser drawer, withdrew a small flashlight, and clicked it on. Then she ran quickly down the staircase.

Dismissing the thought that she should call Clay and let him take care of this, Laurel decided the miscreant would be long gone by the time the sheriff got out here. And she wasn't about to let him get away this time!

Tiptoeing through the kitchen, her heart was hammering wildly as she glanced around for some sort of weapon to take out there with her.

She was undoubtedly dealing with a nutsy, so she wasn't about to confront him unarmed.

Her eyes fell on the long, evil-looking butcher knife lying in the sink drainer, but she discarded that notion quickly. She cut her finger every time she used that knife to slice vegetables. What would it do to her if she tried to slice into a crook with it?

Well, she had to have something, she thought frantically.

Racing over to the kitchen cabinet, she rummaged through the shelves and quickly withdrew a heavy cast-iron frying pan.

Moments later she was wincing her way across the barnyard, trying to creep as quietly as possible. She had forgotten to put on any shoes, and she had to catch herself several times from crying out in pain as she stepped on the jagged rocks lying around.

Where were Dan and Cecile when she needed them?

Her foot came down on something slimy, and she bit her lip to keep from screaming. There was no telling what *that* had been, and she certainly had no inclination to stop and find out.

Again she saw the mysterious figure dart out from behind the grow-out house and wind its way across the open field, heading for the brooder house.

The bright moonlight illuminated his tall, heavy frame, and Laurel's heart began to thud violently.

Maybe it hadn't been such a good idea to face this person alone. He looked powerful and mean. And this frying pan would be a small comfort if she actually had to fight for her life.

But the thought of how this person had been sabotaging her farm quickly lay all her fears to rest and she bravely gathered her nerve.

This time he was not going to get away with it.

Gathering her gown and robe up around her waist, she shot back through the barnyard. She was much smaller than this oaf, and she knew she could outrace him to the brooder house.

Minutes later she came panting to a halt and peered out across the field breathlessly.

Yes, he was still coming this way.

Tucking the heavy frying pan under her arm, she began to inch her way up the tall oak under which he would have to walk if he came anywhere near this direction.

It took several tries before she reached the limb she was seeking, a nice low one she could easily leap from to clobber the criminal before he knew what hit him.

Propping the skillet between two limbs, she tried to regain her breath without being heard. She willed her trembling body to be still.

The branch she was on was fairly vibrating as the culprit's massive form came over a small rise and he paused to look around for a moment.

Seconds later he began to move again. She could hear his footsteps drawing nearer and nearer.

Laurel clamped one hand over her chest to keep her heart from pounding its way out, and shut her eyes tightly.

If he snatched her out of the tree and cut her up into little pieces, she didn't want to witness it.

He was nearly under her branch as he stopped and looked cautiously up into the tree.

Laurel crouched deeper in the foliage and closed her eyes more tightly, silently praying he wouldn't see the dark fabric of her nightgown in the moonlight.

The sound of a man's deep breathing filled the quiet night as he stepped closer under the tree and paused once more.

Laurel could almost feel his evil, penetrating eyes searching through the foliage looking for her. She had never been more frightened in her entire life.

He knew someone was there.

The air crackled with tension as each one waited for the other to make a move.

Suddenly a man's deep voice barked out an order to "come out of that tree," and Laurel went into action.

Leaping out of the tree with a shrill scream, she landed directly on the back of the culprit and started swinging the skillet wildly.

Loud war whoops filled the quiet countryside as she soundly pounded his tall frame and he tried to shake her off his back.

"I'll teach you to mess with me, you pervert," she challenged through gritted teeth as she whacked him painfully across the shoulders and neck. She was past the point of fear now, and she was grimly determined to seek retribution for all the misery he had caused her.

"Cut it out!" he shouted.

"Take that, you imbecile!" She whacked him again.

He let out a bellow of rage, trying to throw her off his back as they both fell to the ground and tumbled around in the dirt.

"And take that!" she ordered again. "And that!" Whack! "And that!" Whack! "And that!"

Her tirade was cut short when he wrapped both his arms around her waist like an iron vise and jerked her to a dead halt.

"I said knock it off, dammit!"

Laurel suddenly recognized the voice.

"Clay!" Her face lit up, and she threw her arms around him in immense relief, her body sagging weakly against his. "Oh, my gosh, Clay. You nearly scared me to death! I thought you were the person who's been creeping around this farm and causing all the problems, and I was scared half out of my wits. I didn't know what in the world I was going to do." She buried her face in his neck and started to sob.

"You were afraid he was going to get the best of *you*?" he asked incredulously. Every inch of his body was throbbing from where she had hit him with the frying pan.

"Yes, I thought he was going to kill me," she bawled. "Why did you scare me like that?" She started to cry harder.

"Honey, I'm sorry."

He was instantly contrite when he saw how upset she was. He tried to soothe her tenderly as he pulled her trembling body close to his own.

"I didn't mean to scare you. I thought *you* were the criminal."

Her tears were wetting the collar of his uniform as she tried to get closer to him. She would have gladly crawled inside him at the moment, she was so frightened and he felt so good, so safe.

"Me!"

"Well, what else could I have thought. I told Dan I was going to stake out the farm tonight. I've been out here since dark watching to see if the Rowden boys were the ones we were looking for," he explained gently.

"Are they?"

"It doesn't look like it. I hadn't seen anyone until I saw you running across the barnyard like a streak of lightning. Of course, I didn't know it was you, or I would have let you know I was out here," he apologized. "What in the hell have you got on?"

He pulled away from her long enough to let his eyes run down the slender length of her scantily clad body. He moaned and pulled her up against him once more. "Your nightgown. Damn!"

"You should have had the decency to let me know what you were going to do," she said crossly, trying to cover herself more decently.

She was becoming just a little put out with him now that the danger had passed.

"I told Dan two days ago what I was going to do," he defended. "We stood right out there in front of the barn and discussed the plan. I assume he never mentioned it? Why are you running around in that flimsy little nightgown?"

He couldn't seem to get his mind off the fact that he had Laurel Henderson in his arms wearing almost nothing; even his body was beginning to betray him now.

"No, Dan didn't say a thing, but he isn't speaking to me too much lately," she confessed. "And I was getting ready to go to bed when I saw you creeping across the yard. That's why I'm running around out here half-naked!"

Clay groaned inwardly. Did she have to keep reminding him?

"You know that was a crazy thing to do, don't you? From now on I want you to promise to call me when something like this comes up again. Okay?" He looked at her sternly.

"I promise," she vowed, her eyes as round as silver dollars.

She would be more than happy to leave that sort of thing up to him from now on.

"All right. Now, why isn't Dan speaking to you lately?" he asked calmly.

"Because I practically accused him of being the one who turned the dog loose in the grow-out house."

"Oh, Laurel." Clay groaned. "When I mentioned that to you about Dan the other day, I was just discussing the possibilities. I didn't want you to run home and accuse him without any evidence."

"I didn't. I had already accused poor Dan of letting Tramp loose in the grow-out house before I ever talked to you."

She sat up and reached for the handkerchief he had dragged out of his back pocket.

"You mean, the thought that Dan might have something to do with all this trouble had occurred to you before I mentioned it?"

"Yes." She sighed and blew her nose. "And you want to hear something even more far-fetched? Now I'm beginning to suspect Cecile might be in on it too."

"Cecile?" Clay let out a low whistle. "What makes you think that?"

"I saw them together tonight . . . taking a moonlight walk."

Clay chuckled. "Wow, what damning evidence."

"No, you don't understand. Cecile has always babbled endlessly about the men she dates, and she has never said one word to me concerning Dan." Laurel cocked her head and looked at Clay expectantly. "Don't you think that sounds a little suspicious?"

"No. I think it sounds like two single people taking a walk in the moonlight." He laughed again.

Laurel shook her head. "I don't think so. I heard them laughing, and it sounded to me like they were . . . well, you know . . . close."

Clay tipped her face up to meet his in the soft rays of the moonlight. "Would it bother you if Dan and Cecile were . . . close?"

"No, not at all," she protested. "If you're trying to imply that I might have an interest in Dan other than as a good friend, you're wrong. I told you that the other night. Dan is a wonderful man, but I'm not in love with him."

He grinned at her boyishly. "I'm glad to hear that."

"Really? Why?" She narrowed her eyes and looked at him with suspicion.

This just might be the perfect time to ask him if he would be interested in having an affair.

"Why?" He looked a little embarrassed that she would question him on his hasty answer. "I don't know."

"What kind of answer is that?" she prompted.

"What do you want me to say?"

"Well, you and I have been friends for a long time," she reminded him. "I feel like I've known you for practically all of my life."

"Yeah, I feel that way about you too," he agreed.

"You also said you and Bea weren't necessarily serious about each other, didn't you?" She continued.

"That's right. Not on my part at least."

"Are you involved . . . I mean, seriously, with anyone else?"

Clay thought for a moment. "Nope. Not that I can think of."

"You're sure?"

He looked at her and grinned. "I think I'd probably remember if I were, and I don't, so I must not be."

"Then would you mind if I ask you to do me a big favor?" She rushed on before she lost her nerve completely.

"I told you, I'm doing everything within my power to help you with those damn turkeys," Clay said with a sigh.

"I'm not talking about the farm," she said, dismissing him. "This is of a more personal nature. But before I ask you, I want you to be aware that it's something I wouldn't ask of just anyone. I want you to know that. I've thought it all through carefully, and I'm convinced that you are the only logical one to help me with my problem."

"You have more 'problems' than any one person I've ever met," he said, chuckling. "But go ahead and ask your favor."

Clay studied her solemn features in the moonlight. Whatever the favor was, it apparently meant a lot to her. He realized he was being foolish, but there wasn't anything he wouldn't do for her, and he knew it.

She tried to find her voice but failed.

"Well?"

The silence lengthened painfully.

Clay leaned over and tipped her face upward. "Laurel?"

Swallowing hard, she grinned weakly. "Would you be interested in having an affair with me?"

CHAPTER SEVEN

Clay's smile was complacent as he crossed his arms behind his head and lay back to gaze at the star-studded sky.

"Sure, Laurel. I'll be happy to take you to the fair. It won't be here for another couple of months, but—"

"Clay!" Laurel stopped him impatiently.

Here she was, offering something that most men only dreamed a woman would offer, and he had misunderstood the invitation!

"I don't want you to go to the *fair* with me."

Clay glanced at her expectantly. "I thought that's what you just asked me."

"No, for heaven's sake!" She felt her face turning pink, and she was glad the moon had slipped behind a stray cloud so he couldn't see her embarrassment.

"I.want you to have an affair with me," she said in exasperation.

The expression in his eyes went totally blank.

"Have a what?"

"An affair . . . you know." She cast her eyes

away from his hurriedly. "I want you to become my lover."

In all the years Laurel Henderson had known Clay Kerwin, she had never seen him move as fast as he did at that particular moment.

He scrambled to his feet and backed away from her as if she were a mad dog foaming at the mouth.

"What's the matter with you?" she asked crossly.

"You'll never believe what I thought you just said."

"What do you think I just said?"

"I thought you said . . ." He laughed self-consciously. "Never mind. Let's start over. What's the favor you want me to do for you?"

"Have an affair with me," she repeated calmly.

"Have an affair with you."

"Yes. I've decided that it was high time I had one," she explained. "I've been so busy over the years, I haven't had time for . . . that sort of relationship, and after giving it a lot of thought, I've come to the conclusion that it will probably be several more years before I'm ready to settle down. I still want to continue my music, and that will take time. I'll probably be in my middle thirties by then. Have you ever heard of a woman in her middle thirties in this day and age not having had at least *one* affair?" she argued, beginning to warm to the subject. "Now, I don't want you to think this is something I'm doing in haste, because it isn't, I can assure you. I've spent the last couple of weeks narrowing down the field of men I think would be the most sensible for me to try my wings with—"

"Try your wings?" he murmured in a stunned voice. He fumbled nervously in his pocket and took out a stick of bubble gum.

"Yes, you know ... I want to soar like an eagle." She smiled tolerantly. "Anyway, I don't know if you're aware of it or not, but this town doesn't have very many eligible prospects for what I'm considering." She paused and looked at him expectantly. "Are you aware of that?"

He shook his head as he unwrapped the gum and absentmindedly popped it in his mouth.

"I didn't think so," she continued. "Well, anyway, I've narrowed down the candidates, and since you and I have known each other a long time and since you're not interested in anyone in particular at this moment ... you did say there is nothing going on between you and Biscuit Beatrice, didn't you?"

Again, he could only nod his head in mute agreement.

"Good. And I've ruled out Cecile, too, although I think you're making a big mistake there," she cautioned. "She would make somebody a lovely wife. She's very talented you know. . . . Clay, are you listening to me?"

He was still nodding his head wordlessly as she glanced up to see if she had his full attention.

"Clay?"

"Huh?"

"Why aren't you saying anything?"

"Because I think you're crazier than a bedbug, that's why."

Her eyes narrowed. "That isn't very nice of you to say," she snapped crossly. "You could think it, but you certainly didn't have to say it."

"Are you sure you didn't hit yourself in the head with that frying pan a few minutes ago?"

"I take this to mean that you're not interested in my proposal," she challenged.

"Come on, Laurel. Let's get serious!"

He was still finding the entire conversation unbelievable as he searched her face for signs of teasing, but to his dismay there was none.

"I hardly think this is something I would joke about. I'm perfectly serious, and if you don't want the job, then I'm going to find someone who does."

She doubted that she really would, but it sounded good. If Clay refused her, then she was back to square one.

"If I want the *job*! This is getting sicker by the minute!"

"All I need from you is a simple yes or no," she said, dismissing him in a grumpy voice. "The last thing I need is a sermon on morality. I'm well aware that what I'm doing is rather cut and dried and completely lacking in morals on my part. But I also explained that I had given a lot of thought to whom I would have an affair with, and your name kept popping up in my mind."

Clay sank back down beside her. "Why me?" he wondered.

"Well, for one thing you're eligible. For another I want to be discreet about the matter, and I know you would be. We've known each other for a very long time, and I feel certain that after the first initial shyness wore off between us . . . I'm sure there's a period of adjustment during these sorts of things, isn't there?" She glanced at him shyly.

"I'm sure there is," he agreed dryly.

"Don't you know for certain?"

Clay shrugged.

"Gee, that's one of the reasons I picked you," she protested. "I thought that since I didn't know what I was doing, you would certainly be experienced enough to carry the ball."

"Oh, I know how to carry the ball," he assured readily.

Laurel snorted. "I'll bet. Anyway, I also figured we could have an affair without feeling like we would owe each other a personal commitment. At the end of the relationship we can both leave with a clear conscience."

"What makes you think I wouldn't ask for a commitment," he parried.

"Because you just wouldn't. Obviously, if you were looking for a permanent relationship, you would have found one years ago. We're neither one exactly spring chickens anymore."

"True, but maybe I don't go in for casual affairs," he argued.

Laurel eyed him skeptically. "You've never had a casual affair?"

"I didn't say that," he pointed out. "I merely

said that maybe I don't go in for casual relationships. Maybe I find them empty and a complete waste of time."

"Well, I wouldn't know about these things, since I've never had one," she admitted.

"I think, if you'll rethink this whole idea, you'll find you really don't want to have an affair, either," he suggested.

"Yes, I do."

"No, you don't."

"Clay." She looked at him in exasperation. "I certainly do. I'm old enough to know if I want to have an affair or not. And I say I do!"

"You're old enough," he conceded. "But apparently you're not wise enough."

"What is that supposed to mean?"

Clay heaved a sigh of impatience. "Hell, Laurel. You don't go running around asking men to have affairs with you."

"I haven't. I've only asked you."

"And what are you going to do if I refuse?"

"*Then* I'll ask someone else."

"See? No responsibility whatsoever," he fumed. "And what happens if I do consent to this ridiculous proposal? What if I find I happen to like the arrangement and want to make it permanent? Then where does that leave me? In a darn mess, that's where!"

"If you don't want to do it, all you have to do is say so," she told him resentfully. "You don't, do you?"

"I didn't say that," he grumbled.

"Well, what *did* you say?"

"Do I have to answer right now?" he asked incredulously.

"Yes. I'm in a hurry."

"You've waited thirty-one years. What's the rush?"

"Because for thirty-one years I've just existed. I want to start living for a change," Laurel pleaded.

Clay reached over and tilted her face toward him. For a few moments he searched her pretty features, wrestling with his weighty decision.

If he refused her offer, he would be leaving her wide open for some other man to take complete advantage of.

If he accepted, he would be leaving himself wide open for a heartbreak he wasn't at all sure he could handle.

Should he grab this chance of a lifetime and pay the piper tomorrow?

Before they both made a whopping mistake, he had to try to talk her out of it one last time.

"Look. Wouldn't you rather reserve this honor for that one special guy in your life? The one you're bound to meet one day?" he coaxed.

"No. You don't seem to understand what I'm saying, Clay. I'm thirty-one years old, and that 'special' guy hasn't come along yet. It's entirely possible that some other woman has gotten to him first and I may not meet him at all."

"You're making me crazy," he groaned.

"Oh, Clay. You don't know how much this means to me," she pleaded. "All I'm asking is this one small favor. I'll take care of everything.

All you have to do is . . ." She searched for the appropriate word.

"Perform?"

"No, that's too tacky," she scolded. "I wouldn't want you to view it that way. Can't you just look on it as helping an old friend out in a pinch?"

He shook his head in disbelief. "Just like that? Out of the clear blue sky we're supposed to have an affair, when thirty minutes ago my only connection to you was tracking down the people responsible for vandalizing your farm?"

"Strange twist of fate, huh?" She smiled encouragingly.

"Very strange."

He leaned back against the trunk of the tree and shut his eyes. He was about to make the biggest mistake of his life, and he wanted to sear the moment on his brain for future recrimination.

"If you don't do it, I'm going to ask Dan," she vowed a few minutes later when he had failed to commit himself.

Laurel knew she wouldn't. She had already ruled Dan out long ago, but it was a reasonable bluff in her estimation.

"I didn't say I wouldn't do it!" Clay protested.

"You will do it?"

"I'm thinking."

They both sat looking up at the starry skies as Clay silently mulled over his decision.

"You realize, I've only kissed you twice in my entire life," he pointed out.

Her heart hammered against her ribs as she

thought what it would be like to kiss this new Clay.

"I'm aware of that."

"Of course, it wouldn't take long to remedy that little problem," he mused. "When you said you'd take care of everything, what does that mean?"

"It means that I will be the one responsible for taking precautions against anything permanent resulting from our . . . arrangement."

"Oh?"

"Yes, I'll go to the doctor first thing in the morning," she promised. "Everything will all be done right."

"Am I allowed to see other women during this . . . uh . . . uh . . ."

"Affair," she prompted. You would think he had never heard the word before now.

"Yes, affair. You said earlier there would be no commitment in this relationship, but I was wondering how you wanted to handle the matter of dating other people while we were seeing each other."

"Well, you're certainly free to do whatever you please," she said curtly. "I won't be seeing anyone else, but the choice as to whether you will or not is strictly up to you." The affair hadn't even started yet, and he was already looking around.

"Yes. Well, I have to give that some thought," he pondered. "And you'll take care of everything?"

"Yes."

He let out a resigned sigh. "Well, it's a dirty job, but I guess someone has to do it." He turned and grinned at her. "We'll have an affair."

She let out her own sigh of relief. "Gee, thanks, Clay. I really appreciate your help."

"Think nothing of it. I'm glad to help out. When do we start?"

It seemed strange to be sitting there discussing this ludicrous arrangement as if they were discussing a flat tire.

"I'd like to get started as soon as possible," she confessed. "Would tomorrow evening be an inconvenience?"

"No, I think I can work it into my schedule. Where do you want it to take place?"

Laurel wasn't quite sure she appreciated his abrupt switch to a rather callous attitude toward the whole situation, but in a way she guessed she had asked for it.

After all, any other man would have thought she was . . . rather loose, to put it mildly.

"I hadn't thought about that," she murmured. "Perhaps a motel?"

"You don't think you and the county sheriff sneaking off to a motel room together for a couple of hours wouldn't lift eyebrows? I thought you wanted to be discreet."

She bit her lower lip pensively. "You're right. The motel's out. How about my place?"

"I'd prefer complete privacy," he argued. "Cecile might walk in on us if we were at your house."

"True." She frowned. "Where do *you* usually go to have an affair?"

"Let's leave me out of this," Clay protested.

"I can hardly do that and still have an affair with you."

"I mean, let's not rely on my experience. You tell me where you want to have your affair, and I'll make sure I'm there on time," he offered.

"How about your house? We could surely have privacy there, and I promise I won't take up much of your time."

He leaned over and picked up his hat from the ground. Dusting it off on his knee, he slapped it back on his head irritably. "This is ridiculous."

"You're not backing out!" She jumped to her feet to confront him. "You said you would do this!"

His eyes seemed to focus unwillingly on the clinging material of her red satin nightgown as the bright moonbeams silhouetted her womanly curves to agonizing perfection.

Try as he might, he couldn't bring himself to put a stop to this fiasco.

"All right. We'll use my house," he agreed reluctantly. "Tomorrow night."

"Thank you. I'm . . . I'm not sure about the procedure. Do I come to you?"

"No, I'll pick you up around seven," he relented. "We'll have a bite to eat, and then I'll take you to my place."

"I'll be ready."

She smiled, trying to put aside the thought of

how many other women he had probably said the same thing to.

Once again his eyes ran longingly over the outline of her softly rounded breasts.

"You know this is absolutely crazy, don't you?"

"I know it's an unusual request," she granted softly. "But it's very important to me, Clay."

"I want you to know something, Laurel." Clay's face turned solemn now as he reached out to touch her cheek. "It's going to be damn hard for me to keep impartial in this thing. I want you to know that right from the beginning. You are the only woman on this earth who could talk me into this, and you'd better believe it."

Clay was being a good friend above and beyond the call of duty, and she was grateful for his help.

Before she could tell him so, he suddenly yanked her to him, and his mouth came down to capture hers roughly.

Her knees turned weak as her arms found their way around the broad expanse of his neck and she willed herself to relax.

After all, if she were going to have an affair with Clay, kissing was certainly going to be involved.

For a second she felt like an ant pressed against Goliath as he kept pulling her closer to his muscular chest.

When he sensed no hesitation from her on returning the kiss, his hold gradually loosened and his tongue gently parted her lips, seeking entrance to the moist warmth he knew awaited him.

The feel of her body molded tightly against his brought forth a low moan from Clay as he murmured her name and deepened the kiss.

For so many years he had only dreamed of this moment, and now that it was here, he drank of her sweet essence like a man dying of thirst.

Laurel was surprised by his undisguised ardor. Already she could feel the proof of his passion as his large hands hesitantly explored her scantily clad body.

Clay Kerwin was a powerful man, and the sheer magnitude of his size and strength threatened to overwhelm Laurel.

She twisted in his arms, murmuring her protests against the pressure of his marauding mouth. It was no longer a teenage Clay stealing a kiss from her beside the sunny banks of a lazy stream but a man who now held her in his tight embrace.

"Clay, please."

She whimpered his name as he buried his hands in her hair and pulled her even closer against his taut frame.

"Laurel, honey . . . I'm sorry."

Clay groaned painfully and broke away from her, his breathing ragged and wanting. He was instantly ashamed of coming on so strong to her, but the feel of her gathered in his arms had made him go a little bit crazy.

She didn't want to offend him or make him think she hadn't been enjoying the kiss, because she most certainly had. So much so, it frightened her. Clay was the first man she could remember who had ever kissed her with such unconcealed desire, and his uninhibited response had taken her completely by surprise.

Giving a shaky laugh, she stepped back from Clay to allow him a few minutes to regain control of his spiraling passion.

He walked over to the trunk of the tree and slapped his hand against it sharply.

A few minutes later he buried his face in his shirt-sleeve and took a couple of deep breaths before he turned to face her once more. "I'm sorry," he said. "I didn't mean to scare you."

"You didn't really scare me," she consoled. "I . . . you just took me by surprise."

"Laurel, I think you'd better reconsider what you're doing," he cautioned in a voice that wasn't quite steady yet. "I'm a pretty demanding man when it comes to making love to a woman, and I don't think you're ready for that sort of man yet."

Shyly she strolled over to where he was standing and placed her hand on his arm. "I want you to make me ready," she told him in a soft voice.

Clay turned and gazed at her longingly. "I don't know if I can be patient enough to get you there without scaring the daylights out of you," he confessed. "You do strange things to me, lady."

He wrapped his arm around her neck and pulled her against his side as they started walking back to the house.

Laurel winced a couple of times as her bare feet encountered foreign objects along the darkened path.

"You tender-footed?"

Clay paused and watched as she sucked in her breath and pranced around the ground.

"Terribly."

Clay shook his head and chuckled. Reaching down, he scooped her up in his arms and proceeded to carry her back to the farmhouse.

"You don't have to do this," she protested, but she had to admit that it felt good to snuggle down against his broad chest.

"I do this for all the women I have affairs with," he said dryly.

"Oh, and were they all barefooted?" she bantered.

"I forgot to look." He grinned. "But I'm sure none of them was as good with a frying pan as you are."

"Flattery, sir, will get you everywhere."

Clay stepped up on the porch and paused. "The door's open. Were you aware of that?"

"Yes, I forgot to close it when I ran out earlier." She paused, and her eyes searched for a light on in the house. It was still as dark as it had been when she'd left earlier. "Cecile must still be walking with Dan."

"It's too hot to sleep," Clay admitted. "She'll probably be in soon."

"It still puzzles me why the two of them are together," Laurel mused. "She told me she was going for a walk because of the heat."

Clay smiled and let her slide suggestively down the front of him as he placed her feet on the floor.

"Maybe Dan has found something to take her mind off the weather."

Their eyes met in the moonlight, and they smiled at each other.

"I suppose you should be getting into bed yourself."

"Yes. It's getting late," she murmured.

Clay's mouth touched hers lingeringly. "You did say you were going to the doctor tomorrow?"

"Oh, yes. I plan on doing that first thing," she assured him in a breathless voice.

"Good. It's still a crazy idea, but if anyone's going to take the angel out of your face, it's going to be me."

"Me, an angel?" Laurel laughed. "I'm far from being an angel, Clay."

"Funny, but I've always thought of you as one."

He leaned over to press his lips against her mouth, making tiny butterflies swarm in her stomach.

Seconds later his mouth captured hers in a series of masterful kisses that left her clinging to him weakly.

He cleared his throat a few moments later and backed away nervously as he reached for the screen door handle. "I think you'd better go in now."

He pushed her gently through the doorway and closed the screen firmly.

Her hand came out to touch the screen as she smiled at him wistfully. "I'll see you tomorrow night."

His large hand reached out to press against her small one. "You bet you will."

And suddenly tomorrow night seemed light-years away for both of them.

CHAPTER EIGHT

Living in a small town could be a real pain sometimes.

Laurel was never more aware of that fact than when she emerged from the doctor's office the following morning.

Oh, Doc Odell hadn't actually said anything when she marched into his office requesting some type of birth control, but he'd certainly turned an uplifted brow in her direction.

"Haven't seen much of you lately," he commented casually as he proceeded to do the necessary examination.

"I know," Laurel said, making small talk. "The farm's been keeping me busy."

"Yes, that's what Paige has been telling me. I spoke to him on the phone just yesterday, and we talked a bit about the farm." Doc paused and looked thoughtful. "You know, I'm a little worried about Paige. He was supposed to meet me for lunch yesterday—we always meet for lunch once a week on the same day—but he wasn't there this week. When I called to see what had happened to him, he acted confused, as if he didn't know what I was talking about."

"He's acted that way with me too," Laurel confessed.

"Well, I don't think we need to be concerned," he said with a chuckle. "He's just getting a little old and forgetful." He peered owlishly at her over the rims of his glasses and changed the subject. "Are you seeing anyone special nowadays?"

She knew he was dying to know what she was up to, but he would just have to form his own conclusions. "Nope. No one special," she replied brightly.

Marvin Odell had treated Laurel since she was just a young girl. He looked upon her as more of a daughter than a mere patient, so she knew he wasn't above trying to give her advice.

"I thought by now that you and Dan might have something serious going in the romance department," he remarked.

"Dan!" Laurel sat up on the table and glared at him soundly. "For heaven's sake! It isn't Dan—" She broke off suddenly.

"Oh?" Doc Odell's face was almost comical in his surprise.

"No . . . I mean, Dan and I aren't seeing each other," she returned nonchalantly. "As I said, I'm not seeing anyone in particular right now."

The doctor's left eyebrow raised a fraction, but he stifled his growing curiosity and went about his business.

"Why, I just supposed you two would get

together now that Sam's gone," he observed offhandedly.

Lying back down on the table, Laurel primly pulled the sheet closer around her. "Well, you supposed wrong. Maybe Cecile and Dan will get together, but not Dan and I."

Cecile had come in the house from her walk with Dan very late the night before. Laurel had debated whether or not to confront her with a barrage of questions but had decided against it. Instead she made a mental note to keep a close eye on the situation for the next few days.

"Dan is a marvelous foreman and a very good friend," Laurel confirmed, "but our relationship is and always will be strictly platonic."

"Hmmmm."

"That's right."

"Don't suppose there's too many eligible men around here for a woman to choose from," he said, trying again. "Only two or three to my knowledge."

Laurel felt herself flush. He was quietly narrowing down the field in his mind.

"I wouldn't know. I really haven't kept count," she said pleasantly.

There were times she resented his kindly meddling in her affairs . . . uh, business!

Whether he approved or disapproved of her projected new life-style, he ended up fitting her with the proper device for birth control. But not without a long sermon on how he viewed the morality of youth nowadays. At least when she left his office thirty minutes later she had what she had come for, and he was still guessing.

139

He was right, of course. Morality wasn't what it should be, but what was a person to do?

Making a quick stop at the market for bread and milk, Laurel dropped her purse in her haste and was delayed for several minutes while she tried to chase the contents of her bag around the floor. She could only hope that she had retrieved all the articles—people were beginning to stare as she crawled from beneath the meat counter with a silly grin on her face, a tube of lipstick clutched in her hand.

At that embarrassing moment she decided that whatever she hadn't found, she would gladly donate to the market.

She was glad to finally get out of there and be on her way home.

Dan was waiting for her when she drove up the farm driveway. She smiled a welcome and told him she would be out to help him clean the brooder house as soon as she changed her clothes.

She hurriedly slipped on a pair of shorts and a lightweight T-shirt and went back outside.

"I'm sorry I'm so late," she apologized as she finally joined Dan.

"No problem," he returned absently, already at work.

Ever since they had exchanged words the other day, Dan had been holding himself in cool reserve. How Laurel wanted to see him return to his old cheerful self.

Neither one had brought up the heated conversation as they went about their daily work, but Laurel had noticed that Dan hadn't stopped by for coffee all week.

Was it possible she had hit on a sore spot when she had accused him of being the one responsible for her recent misfortune?

She desperately wanted to believe that wasn't so.

It was several hours later when Laurel and Dan finished their chores and closed the door to the brooder house. They walked back to the barn to store their tools and wash up. Slumping against a bale of hay, Laurel wiped at her damp forehead and accepted one of the cold drinks Dan handed her from a cooler he kept in the corner.

"This heat is horrible!" she complained as she took a long drink.

The two sat drinking their colas in silence.

Deciding to try to break the tension between them, Laurel spoke. "About the other day, Dan . . ."

"I don't think we should get into that again," he said, stopping her curtly.

"But I want you to know I'm sorry for what I implied," she said, trying again.

"Maybe you shouldn't be." Dan picked up a hundred-pound sack of cattle feed and hoisted it over his shoulder with ease.

"What's that supposed to mean?"

"It means, if I were in your place, I'd probably have the same suspicions you have," he granted. "Let's just leave it at that."

"I don't want you to be mad at me."

"I'm not mad."

Laurel sighed, feeling helpless. She watched Dan shift the feed sack to his other shoulder, and she couldn't help but notice how well built he was for a man his age. There wasn't a dry thread on his blue work shirt, but that couldn't detract from his rippling muscles flexing under the fabric.

Laurel shook herself and tried to center her attention back on the conversation.

"Have you seen Cecile today?"

The question was intended to be conversational, but instead it came out almost as an accusation.

Dan's face turned guarded. "No, I haven't seen her all day. Why do you ask?"

"Just wondering. Do you have any plans for this evening?"

Again Dan's face was noncommittal. "Not really."

"I'm going to be gone for a while. Can you look after things around here?"

"I suppose so." It was his turn to be inquisitive. "Where are you off to?"

"Clay and I are going to have dinner together," she murmured. "Business . . . of sorts."

"Oh?"

"Yes, oh! Is there anything wrong with that?"

All of a sudden she had this overwhelming feeling that he knew what she was up to.

Dan shrugged and readjusted the feed sack.

"Not that I know of. I'll take care of things here."

He pushed past her and disappeared through the barn doorway before she could say another word.

Slumping back on a bale of hay, Laurel sighed.

He was still put-out with her.

Just like a typical man. Let him catch a woman on one of her slightly off days and he runs around and pouts about it for weeks.

Well, she had another man to think about right now. Clay would be over to pick her up in a couple of hours, and if she didn't get herself cleaned up, she could kiss his companionship good-bye for the evening too.

There must be something in the air around this town that made the men suddenly overpoweringly male.

Either that or she was becoming oversexed, Laurel glumly decided.

When Clay knocked on the back door that evening, he looked like a bottle of Scotch to a dry sailor.

"You're right on time," she complimented him as she held the screen door open for him to come in.

It was the first time in a long time she had seen him out of uniform. Tonight he was wearing a pair of casual slacks and a crisply ironed short-sleeved shirt, the color almost matching the dark blue of his eyes. His hair was jet-black, and his clean, masculine fragrance washed over her as he entered the house. In his hand was a small bouquet of late-blooming summer wild flowers.

"I saw these along the road on the way over," he offered lamely. "Thought you might enjoy them."

"They're beautiful," she praised. "I'll put them in water."

She took the flowers and walked over to the sink to fill a small vase. "I'm surprised they're still so lovely," she marveled. "It's so dry right now, everything is dying on the vine."

Laurel glanced shyly over at Clay. She had been vacillating all day between eager anticipation of the evening and dread of the hour of its arrival. What with second thoughts about her rash proposal and the sinking suspicion that Clay must believe she had come unhinged, she had been tempted many times during the afternoon to call him and cancel the clandestine arrangement.

But some small demon kept her from following through, and now he was standing in the kitchen facing her.

"We could sure use a good rain," he agreed.

Setting the vase with the vividly colored flowers in the middle of the table, she stood back and admired them one final time.

"There. Aren't they nice?"

"Real nice."

Clay seemed to be a little edgy himself tonight, she noted with relief. Well, it wasn't every day he found himself in this rather unique situation . . . or at least she hoped not.

"Well, if you're ready . . ." He looked at her expectantly.

"Yes, I'm ready. Just let me grab my purse." Seconds later she returned, and they walked out to his car.

"Hope you don't mind, but I brought the patrol car," Clay apologized as he helped her in the passenger seat.

"No, not at all."

"Buck's covering for me tonight, but you never know when he might need some help."

Clay walked around to the driver's side and got in. He started the engine and glanced over at her. "I hope you like picnics."

She smiled and cast a wary eye at the blouse and skirt she had worn. "I love picnics," she confided.

"If you'd rather go somewhere else . . ." he prompted.

"Oh, no. A picnic is fine." She smiled her approval once more.

"I just thought it would give us a little more privacy than a restaurant would," he reasoned. "I thought we could talk and sort of reacquaint ourselves before . . ." He paused and nervously fumbled in his pocket for a piece of bubble gum. "So I had Bea pack some chicken and potato salad," he finished hurriedly.

"Oh. Beatrice Mosely fixed our dinner?"

Laurel wasn't about to eat *her* biscuits.

"Yeah, she's a real good cook."

"Yes, so you've said." At least a hundred times, she thought snidely.

The CB radio crackled, and Buck Gordon's voice came over the receiver. "Clay, have you got your ears on?"

Clay reached down and picked up the microphone as he turned onto the main highway.

"Yeah, Buck."

"Sorry to bother you, but I've got a problem."

"Oh?" Clay frowned.

"I've been busier than a one-legged dog at a flea convention," the deputy complained good-naturedly. "I'm working a minor accident over here by the café, and I just got a call from Ernestine and Howard Raybern's neighbors."

"Oh, hell. Are those two at it again?" Clay unwrapped the stick of bubble gum and popped it in his mouth.

"Yeah. Howard's been tippin' the bottle again, and Ernestine's chasing him around the outside of the house with a broom. Neighbors want someone to go over there and quiet them down."

"Well, I'm not that far from their place. I'll swing over there and see what I can do."

He cast an apologetic glance toward Laurel.

"Shore appreciate it, boss."

Buck signed off as Clay made a sweeping U-turn on the highway and headed the patrol car back in the direction from which they had just come.

"This won't take but a few minutes," Clay promised as they gunned their way down the blacktop road.

Howard and Ernestine Raybern were a colorful old couple who lived at the outskirts of town. Howard had a tendency to overdrink. Ernestine had a tendency to either lock him out of the house for days or else whip the living daylights out of him if she happened to be in the mood.

Apparently she had chosen the latter this evening.

As they bumped along the rutted drive leading up to the farmhouse, Clay assured Laurel once more that his business would be finished in a matter of minutes.

"Stay in the car," he warned as they pulled up before the clapboard house. He shut off the car's engine.

"Is this going to be dangerous?" she asked worriedly.

They both watched as an irate woman wielding a huge broom chased a harried-looking man around the yard.

They streaked by the patrol car shouting obscenities at each other and disappeared around the side of the house.

"Only to me," he grumbled. "Sorry about the language."

Laurel grinned. "Colorful, isn't it?"

"Lady, you ain't heard nothin' yet," he quipped, and opened his car door.

Moments later he disappeared behind the house in search of the warring couple.

All three came barreling around the side in a dead heat five minutes later.

The woman was still chasing the man, and Clay was chasing the woman.

"Ernestine! I said put that broom down and stop in the name of the law!" Clay roared.

All three ran back around the house as Laurel watched with mortified fascination.

She had no idea that Clay's job was so exerting.

When the trio came in view again, the positions had been reversed. The woman was now chasing both men, intermittently whacking them about the shoulders with her broom.

"I'm warning you, Ernestine—" Clay's words were obliterated by another sound thump of the broom on the top of his head.

Laurel could no longer stand by and watch Clay being pulverized by this crazy woman's actions.

She bounded out of the car and jumped into the middle of the melee, trying to force the broom away from Ernestine.

For a few moments it was a fierce shouting match between the four as Clay frantically tried to separate the two women.

"Howard, grab Ernestine!" Clay reached over, picked Laurel up by the waist, and swung her out of harm's way as the broom came down on his broad back once more.

"Damn! Get that broom away from her, Howard, before I haul you both in," he bellowed.

Howard seized the moment to snatch the bristled weapon out of his wife's hands and run toward the safety of the house with it.

Seconds later the front door slammed loudly and Howard disappeared.

Clay grabbed Ernestine's skirt tail as she proceeded to follow her husband into the house. "Now hold on just a minute."

Her temper finally beginning to cool, Ernestine screeched to a halt and cast her eyes sheepishly down on the ground in front of her.

"Ain't got much time for visitin', Sheriff. Got a pan of bread in the oven."

"You had enough time to try to beat my brains out," he snapped. "What's all the ruckus about this time?"

"Howard came home a drinkin' again, Sheriff. You know I'm a peaceful, law-abiding citizen, and I don't cause no trouble except when Howard comes home stewed to the gills," she whined. "You wouldn't haul me to jail for that, would you?" She peered up at his six-foot two-inch frame and cringed.

"That's no reason to try to decapitate the sheriff!" Laurel snapped.

"Didn't mean to hit the sheriff," Ernestine said with a pout. "He just got in the line of fire."

Clay walked over and put a glowering Laurel back in the car, shutting the door firmly.

"*You* sit in this car and don't move a muscle."

"But I was only trying to help—"

"Not one muscle!" He glared at her sternly. "Now, come on, Ernestine. Me and you and Howard are going to have us a little talk."

Laurel had to admit she felt sorry for the old woman as Clay took her firmly by the arm and led her purposefully into the house.

At that moment Sheriff Clay Kerwin was a force she sure wouldn't want to reckon with.

It was at least twenty minutes later when Clay emerged from the house and got back in the car.

"Everything settled down?" Laurel inquired.

"Yeah." Clay made a hurried assessment of her slender frame. "Did you get hurt in the fracas?"

"No," she scoffed. "I'm fine."

"I'm personally going to turn you over my knee and tan your hide if I ever catch you jumping in the middle of a brawl like that again," he threatened. "Don't you know you could get yourself hurt doing things like that?"

"I couldn't stand by and watch Ernestine flog you to death," she shot back indignantly.

"I can handle Ernestine," he pointed out. "I've been holding my own with her ever since I took office."

"You mean this happens frequently?"

"I'm out here more times than I care to be," he acknowledged with disgust as he started the car and backed out the drive. "That Ernestine is about as wicked with a broom as you are with the frying pan."

Laurel blushed. Poor Clay must be black and blue from the abuse he had taken in the last twenty-four hours.

"Where are we going?" she asked a few minutes later as the car turned back on the open highway.

"I thought we'd go out by the river and have our picnic."

Laurel was glad they were going somewhere peaceful. After the last hour she would welcome the calm.

A few minutes later Clay pulled the patrol car under a large hickory tree. Glancing around the familiar surroundings, Laurel felt a rush of gratitude that he had thought to bring her to a spot where they had spent many hours of their teenage years.

Somehow it would make this evening so much easier. It seemed that every day she was learning what a thoughtful man Clay Kerwin could be.

"You remember this place?" he asked quietly.

Her smile was tender. "Sure. If I'm not mistaken, I think I received my first kiss here."

Clay chuckled. "I was hoping you'd remember the exact spot for that reason alone."

"A girl doesn't forget her first kiss," she told him.

His eyes ran over her hungrily. "Good. I hope she won't forget the next one she gets out here, either."

He pulled her over to him and touched his mouth to hers briefly.

"That kiss wouldn't be too hard to forget," she chided, wishing he would kiss her the way he had last night.

Again his mouth toyed with hers lightly, sending goose bumps all over her warm skin.

"If I kissed you the way I'd like to right now, we would never get to eat our dinner," he parried. "I'm getting hungry. How about you?"

She could read an entirely different meaning into his words if she let herself, and she decided to test his endurance.

"Ummm." Her tongue touched his fleetingly. "A little."

"What are you hungry for, Laurel Henderson?"

Again his mouth took hers gently.

"That depends. You're the one who's planned the menu."

For some reason it felt perfectly natural to be here in his arms ... teasing him, and Laurel was enjoying it immensely.

His breath caught as she wrapped her arms around him and kissed him the way she had been wanting to all evening.

For a moment it caught him by surprise, then he groaned and pulled her closer to him, returning the kiss unabashedly.

They exchanged kiss for kiss, acquainting themselves with the taste and feel of each other, forgetting all previous thoughts of their picnic.

Finally he let out a ragged breath and reluctantly set her aside. "I think I had better get to that fried chicken while I'm still able to."

The evening was young, and he still had plenty of time to complete their mission. The last thing he wanted to do was rush her or make her feel uneasy about their new relationship.

Laurel heard her stomach growl as Clay stole one more brief kiss and opened his car door. She had to admit that she was getting hungry too.

"I'll get the picnic basket if you'll spread the blanket out on the ground. We haven't got much daylight left," he noted.

Laurel took the blanket from him. She had just found a nice grassy spot to place it on when Clay returned with a funny look on his face.

"What's wrong?"

"I hope you're not too hungry."

"Why?"

He grinned sheepishly. "I guess my mind was on other things when I was getting ready to leave the house. I left the picnic basket sitting on the kitchen table."

"Honest?"

"Honest."

They both laughed nervously.

"Well, I think I have a candy bar in my purse we can share," she offered.

"Is it gooseberry?" he bantered, then chuckled at his own private joke and came to join her on the blanket.

"No. Do they make gooseberry?"

"I don't think so." Or at least he sure hoped not.

She rummaged in her purse and found the candy bar, which they shared in contented companionship.

They found themselves talking of days gone by and friendships they had shared in school. It seemed like old times sitting by the bank of the river talking together as the evening descended into dusk.

Before they knew it, they were touching more often, and their eyes would meet for longer periods of time before they were able to break their gazes.

It occurred to Laurel that instead of going back to Clay's house, he had thoughtfully brought her out here to make love to her. This way it would seem more natural . . . less self-seeking.

Well, it seemed only fitting. He'd given her her first kiss here under this tree. . . .

"Did you go to see Doc Odell today?" Clay's deep voice interrupted her thoughts.

She felt her face coloring as she tried to avoid his gaze.

"Yes."

"Everything go all right?"

"Yes," she confirmed.

Once again Clay chuckled as he wrapped his arm around her and pulled her over to join him. They both lay back on the blanket and looked up in the darkening sky.

"Going to be a full moon tonight," he commented lazily.

"Ummm." She was acutely aware of how good he smelled this evening.

"Lover's moon," he pointed out.

She murmured her response again and snuggled down closer in his arms.

She was grateful he wasn't trying to rush things. He seemed to be taking his time and enjoying her company.

"Did I ever tell you what a crush I had on you all the years we went to school together?" he murmured as his arm tightened possessively around her shoulders.

Her pulse fluttered at his almost bashful confession.

"I believe you mentioned it the other day. Why didn't you ever let me know?" she chided.

"Would it have made a difference to you back then?"

"Probably not," she confessed. "You were just
. . . Clay. I really never thought of you as a man."

"Well, at that time I wasn't much of one," he
conceded, and rolled over to face her. "But 'I've
come a long way, baby.' "

"I can see that."

Close to nine thousand miles, in her opinion.

Her arms found their way around his neck as
his lips came coaxingly down to meet hers.

Forcing her lips open with his tongue, he
explored the sweetness of her mouth with a
smothered groan. The moment he had been
waiting for most of his life was drawing near,
and he began to tremble in anticipation.

"You're trembling," Laurel soothed, caressing
the back of his neck tenderly.

"Yeah." He laughed nervously. "Aren't you
supposed to be the one doing that?"

"I suppose I should," she admitted, letting
her fingers slide through the rich, thick texture
of his hair.

She hated to let him know she trusted him so
implicitly. It would probably go straight to his
head. With any other man Laurel knew she
would have backed out hours ago, but not with
Clay.

Her fingers found the buttons of his shirt,
and she timidly undid the first three.

"Do you mind?" she asked hesitantly.

Clay took her hands and helped her unfasten
the remaining ones. "You have my permission
to do anything you like," he granted in a husky
voice.

Her hands gently touched the sleek bronze skin that covered his broad chest.

His stomach was ridged with tight muscles that became even tighter as she ran her hand lightly over his bare torso.

"You are beautiful," she whispered in a voice filled with reverence.

"Thank you. You are too." His gaze was limpid as his blue eyes finally captured hers. "I really mean that, Laurel. I think you're one of the prettiest women I've ever seen."

"Do you mind if I take your shirt off?" she asked timidly.

He shook his head wordlessly as he helped her pull the shirt off. As her eyes searched his broad, handsome chest, Laurel caught sight of a thin scar climbing along the left side of his rib cage.

"Who did this horrible thing to you?" she asked sharply. A surge of overwhelming protectiveness filled her as her fingers tenderly examined the one imperfection on his beautiful body.

He chuckled at her cross tone. "That one? Well, now, let me think. I believe that was given to me by a fellow who didn't quite see my way of thinking on a couple of issues."

"What were you arguing about?"

"Several different points. I thought he needed an attitude adjustment, and he thought I needed one. Since he was the one who had the knife in his hand, he was just a little more convincing than I was."

"Oh, Clay!"

"Hey, no sweat. He eventually came around to my point of view," Clay said. "We almost killed each other in the process, but it all worked out."

"Does he still live around here?"

"No. He left town shortly after that."

Her eyes went back to his bronzed physique. "Why, there are several scars. . . ."

On closer examination Clay's body showed signs of injuries from the last few years, and it nearly tore her heart out.

"How have you managed to stay alive?" she murmured, touching her mouth to the new wound she had just discovered.

"I'm afraid it all comes with the job." His breath caught and held as her tongue touched his warm skin. "Oh, lady. If I had any idea scars turned you on so—"

"I think they're horrible!" she scolded. "Why don't you take better care of yourself?"

It pained her to think he would be subject to such violence and she couldn't do a thing about it.

He chuckled again and took both her hands in his. The blue of his eyes deepened as their gazes met and held. "Listen. When we get to know each other a little better, I have another scar I'd like you to 'kiss and make well.' "

"Where is it? I'll do it right now," she offered warmly.

"Ummm . . . I don't think so. . . ."

"Is it a bad one?"

"Let's just say it almost made the difference

in me being a rooster or a hen," he teased, and chuckled out loud when he saw her face go a bright pink. "I'm sorry. I shouldn't tease you like that."

"No, you shouldn't," she agreed with embarrassment.

His smile grew tender. "You don't have to be shy around me. I want us to get to know everything there is to know about each other's bodies."

His mouth covered hers in a consuming, powerful kiss, dissolving all thoughts of other conversation.

A fire suddenly sprang up and ignited between them. Moments later Laurel found herself clinging weakly to him as his hands began to undo the buttons on her blouse.

"Clay, I . . ." This thing was beginning to move along much faster than she had anticipated, and she grew uneasy. Maybe she was doing something wrong, and he wanted to get it over with as quickly as possible.

"Don't be afraid. I would never hurt you, Laurel. You know that." He gave her another long, reassuring kiss as one of his hands lightly caressed her bare midriff.

"I'm not afraid. I was just wondering if I was doing something to displease you."

"Displease me?" He laughed again in a shaky voice. "No, you're not displeasing me in the least . . . that's the problem."

A few moments later he groaned, and whispered a ragged set of instructions in her ear. Laurel obediently reached for her purse.

She fumbled around the contents, then paused and pushed him gently away from her.

"Wait a minute . . ."

He lifted his head and looked at her, puzzled. "What's the matter?"

"I can't find it."

"Find what?"

"The thing the doctor gave me this morning." She shook her purse and peered in the bag worriedly. "I know it's in here somewhere. . . ."

Clay slid off her and watched as she rummaged through the articles of her purse once more.

"I can't find it," she mused fretfully, digging deeper.

"Oh, good grief! Here, let me look." Clay snatched the purse and dumped the entire contents out on the blanket.

After a thorough five-minute search they both came up empty-handed once more.

"Are you *sure* you didn't leave it lying some-where at home?" he prompted.

"Of course, I'm sure," she said with a moan. "It must have fallen out when I dropped my purse at the grocery store."

"Damn, Laurel." Clay leaned back on his knees and took a deep breath. "Couldn't you have lost anything but that!"

"I'm sorry, Clay. I know it was stupid, but I didn't do it on purpose," she pleaded. "It was an accident."

She wasn't experienced in this sort of thing, but she knew this interruption of their plans was bound to be hard on Clay.

"Well, what are we going to do?" She peered at him expectantly.

"Other than sit here and breathe heavily? Nothing. Absolutely nothing," he predicted glumly, and started to rebutton his shirt.

"Nothing?"

"Look. Let's not make this any harder than it is. I'm not carrying anything with me." He raised his hands hopelessly.

"Oh, dear." She bit her lip. "Well, I suppose we'll have to postpone . . . things until tomorrow evening."

She offered him an encouraging smile and brightened considerably. So, they had encountered a minor setback. An affair was something that shouldn't be rushed, anyway.

"Tell you what. First thing tomorrow morning I'll start all over again."

"You're going back to Doc Odell again?" he asked incredulously.

"No, that would be too embarrassing," she admitted. "But I can run down to the drugstore and buy something over the counter. Don't worry. I'll take care of it."

Clay grunted something under his breath and stuffed his shirt tails back in his trousers.

"You're not mad at me, are you?" she inquired uneasily.

"No. I suppose this could happen to anyone," he grumbled.

She stood up and wrapped her arms around his neck affectionately. "I promise, tomorrow night will be different."

"It sure will. I can't make it tomorrow night," he confessed.

"Why not?" She tried to keep the disappointment hidden in her voice but failed.

"I'm sorry, honey, but I already have another date for tomorrow night," he confessed.

"You do?"

"Look, I made this date before I started seeing you. I can break it if you want me to, but she's going to wonder why. If you're really serious about wanting to keep our relationship discreet . . ."

He let her finish the sentence in her own mind.

"No, I don't want you to break the date. I told you from the beginning that you could date whoever you wanted." Her eyes narrowed. "Who is it, and where are you going?"

He grinned at her lack of aplomb. "It's with Cecile, and I've volunteered my services over at Freistatt again this year. And it won't actually be a date," he went on. "I'll be on duty most of the evening. When I mentioned my plans to her the other night, she asked if I minded if she tagged along. She said she hadn't been to the Ernte-Fest in several years."

"She hasn't," Laurel confirmed. "And I think it's very nice of you to take her with you this year."

Laurel didn't *really* think it was nice of him to take her sister. She would much prefer it be herself, but she felt an obligation to be polite.

Clay leaned down and tipped her face up to

meet his with one finger. "Hey. Why don't you come with us?"

"No, I wouldn't want to interfere," she said evasively. "But I imagine I will end up going. I love that festival."

"Good. If you do come, I'll make it a point to look you up and have a polka with you," he encouraged.

"That's sounds nice. Dan and I will probably run into you sometime during the night."

"Dan!" Clay frowned.

"Yes. I think I'll ask him to take me."

"I thought you weren't interested in Dan," he said curtly.

"And I thought you weren't interested in Cecile."

"I'm not. She's the one who asked me to take her, not the other way around."

"You're absolutely sure you're not interested in my sister?" Laurel studied him suspiciously.

"Do you want a sworn affidavit? No, I'm not interested in your sister."

"I'm not interested in Dan, either, but I'm still going to ask him to take me to the Ernte-Fest."

Clay's hands dropped from her shoulders reluctantly. "All you have to do is say the word and I'll break the date with Cecile and take you," he reminded curtly. "I'd rather do it that way, anyway."

"No," she refused, unwilling to admit to herself that she was jealous of his date with her own sister. "We'll have our date the following night

. . . if you're not tied up with Cecile that night too."

He sighed impatiently. "I'll pick you up around seven."

Clay wasn't about to force this issue with her. If he could be with Laurel Henderson on any terms, then he would let her dictate those terms.

"Fine. I should have everything under control by then," she promised as they picked up the blanket and walked to the car. "We'll get this affair rolling day after tomorrow."

"Great. Now I'll go home and stand in a cold shower for an hour, eat a piece of my birthday gooseberry bread, and go to bed . . . alone."

"Good, because absolutely nothing will go wrong this time," she assured him in a relieved voice. "I promise."

At the moment he wasn't inclined to believe her, but considering the choices, he forced himself.

CHAPTER NINE

"I understand you're going to the Ernte-Fest with Clay tonight."

Laurel sat across the kitchen table from Cecile the next morning and took a cautious sip of her hot coffee. Because of the heat, Cecile was up early and didn't appear to Laurel to be in the best of moods.

"When is something going to be done about the air conditioner?" she complained, totally ignoring her sister's question.

Impatiently tapping a cigarette out of an almost empty package, Cecile stuck the tip end in her mouth and lit it.

"Dan said that because of the extreme heat, the electrician is running behind," Laurel explained. "It shouldn't be too much longer before he gets around to us."

"I sure hope not. I don't know why you don't just call another electrician. If the man can't handle his job, I can't see any future in waiting around for him," she snapped.

"There are not that many electricians in town," Laurel snapped back. "He'll get to us when he can."

They sat for a few tense moments, each one drinking her coffee.

Laurel could understand Cecile's short temper. It was bound to be frustrating sitting around day after day with nothing to do. Her sister helped out with the housework, and lately she had taken a bit more interest in the running of the farm, but there were still far too many idle hours on Cecile's hands.

Combined with the stifling heat, it was no wonder she was more snappish than usual.

"Are you looking forward to your date with Clay?" Laurel tried once more to make casual conversation and satisfy her own nagging curiosity.

"I suppose so. Clay's a nice guy."

"Yeah, he is." For a moment her thoughts skipped back to the night before and what had almost happened between her and Clay Kerwin. Drat her rotten luck!

"Are you going over to Freistatt tonight?" Cecile's voice brought her back to the present.

"Maybe. I thought I might ask Dan if he would take me."

Her sister glanced up sharply. "Dan?"

Laurel's eyes narrowed. "Yes. Any objections?"

It would be interesting to see if Cecile said anything about her moonlight walk with Laurel's foreman.

"Objections?" It seemed to Laurel that her sister's laugh was forced. "Why should I object to you seeing Dan?"

"Well, it's not as though I'm 'seeing' him,"

Laurel pointed out. "In fact, I think he's still upset with me over the misunderstanding we had the other day. But I thought this might be a nice time for me to make amends with him."

She watched Cecile's face to see how she was taking the news, but her sister was trained to keep her face expressionless if she so chose.

And at the moment that's exactly what she was choosing to do.

"I'm sure Dan would enjoy the evening out. Maybe we'll all see each other there," Cecile noted.

Laurel's pulses leapt at the thought of being with Clay again tonight. "That would be nice. I'll check with Dan and see if he can ask one of the neighborhood boys to keep an eye on the farm while we're gone."

"By the way, I saw those two Rowden boys cutting across the fields late last night," Cecile told her.

"When?"

"I was looking out the window about midnight or so and I saw Jake and Eddy running in the direction of their farm."

Laurel looked pensive. Dan had not reported any new vandalism to the farm this morning, but she hadn't actually seen him yet. And Laurel had to admit that it wasn't really all that unusual for the brothers to cut across her land on their way home, but Clay's earlier suspicions teased at her mind.

Had they been up to no good, and Dan just hadn't discovered the evidence yet?

"I wonder what they were doing?" Laurel mused.

"Who knows. You know boys their age."

The words were no sooner out of her mouth than there was a sharp rap on the back door.

Both sisters glanced up as Dan opened the door and stepped in the kitchen.

"Hi, Dan!" Cecile's grouchy mood disappeared into thin air.

Laurel couldn't help but notice that Dan's smile was much more than just a polite grin.

"Hello, Cecile."

For a moment the two of them looked lingeringly at each other until Dan suddenly remembered where he was.

"Uh . . . we have some more trouble, Laurel."

Laurel pushed back from the table and faced him apprehensively. "What now?"

"Someone's tipped over the feed bins," he announced gravely.

"The feed bins! Oh, no!"

Laurel couldn't think of a worse headache. The heavy feed bins were large and cumbersome. If someone had tipped them over, it meant they were damaged beyond repair and would have to be replaced quickly.

"When did they do that?"

"Sometime last night. I was a little late getting over here this morning," he glanced guiltily at Cecile, "so I was late making my rounds. I found the damage a few minutes ago."

"Those Rowden boys!" Laurel slammed her hand down on the kitchen table. "That must be what they were doing when Cecile saw them last night."

Dan glanced at Cecile. "You saw Jake and Eddy last night?"

"Yes, they were running across the field around midnight," she verified.

Dan shook his head irritably. "You wait until I get my hands on those young hoodlums!"

"What about the feeders?" Laurel prompted. "How bad is it?"

"All four will have to be replaced."

Laurel groaned. "I'll get dressed and be out in a few minutes."

She hurried out of the kitchen, leaving Dan and Cecile alone.

If anything was going on between those two, she didn't have time to concern herself with it today.

When Laurel joined Dan and Cecile to face the havoc twenty minutes later, she wanted to cry as she viewed the callous destruction of the massive aluminum feeders that stood beside each grow-out house and the brooder house. They were crushed beyond repair, and feed was thrown around in wild disarray beside each building.

Since this was the crucial source by which the turkeys were fed, something had to be done to correct the vandalism immediately.

"How do you suppose they did this?" Laurel fretted as she knelt down and ran her hand through some of the scattered feed.

"They would have had to use a truck to pull

them over," Dan guessed. "The bins were just filled yesterday, and there was too much feed in them for someone to tip over by hand."

"A truck! Well, that rules out Eddy and Jake. Neither one of them keep a job long enough to buy any sort of vehicle." Laurel shook her head in disgust. Another dead end. "Wouldn't you have heard a truck pull up in the yard?"

Dan looked at Cecile. "Normally I would have."

"Normally? What does that mean?" Laurel looked at Dan sharply. "Didn't you stay around last night to watch things while I was gone?"

"Sure, I was here, but I took a walk down by the pond and stayed there for a while," he said, defending himself. "It was late when I came back, and since I'd checked the turkeys earlier, I went on home."

"Wouldn't the turkeys have made a racket if someone was disturbing them?" Cecile suggested.

"They certainly should have," Laurel reasoned curtly. She turned to face Dan once more. "You didn't hear anything unusual?"

"Not a thing."

For Laurel that was extremely hard to believe, and she couldn't help but let it show on her face.

"Are you accusing me of neglecting my job again?" Dan challenged.

"If the shoe fits, wear it," Laurel snapped.

"I'm getting a little tired of your veiled accusations," Dan said calmly. "If you have something to say, come right out and say it."

"Dan . . ." Cecile called his name softly and shot him a warning look.

169

Once again Laurel was faced with the decision to confront Dan and get her nagging suspicions out in the open once and for all, or let the matter lie.

For a moment it was eye-to-eye combat between Dan and Laurel, but she finally whirled on her heel and marched back in the direction of the house without saying another word.

"Took a walk down by the pond, indeed!" she muttered as she tramped along the dusty path.

He had been with Cecile, no doubt. And they were so engrossed in each other, they failed to hear a truck pull in the farmyard and virtually destroy half her farm!

That was highly unlikely in Laurel's opinion, and now she wished she had told him so.

Storming into the house in a fit of temper, she had just decided to report this newest violation of her property to the county's highly inept sheriff when the phone rang.

"What!"

"Laurel?" Clay's voice sounded puzzled.

"Do you have any idea what they've done now?" she accused, close to tears of frustration.

"Who?"

"*Who!*" She stomped her foot angrily. "I don't know who! That's what you're being paid to find out!"

"Hey, whoa. Let's back up and start all over." His voice took on a concerned edge this time. "What's going on out there?"

Laurel sank down on the nearest chair and started to bawl.

She was hot, tired, and sick to death of running a turkey farm that was rapidly going straight down the tubes.

"Laurel? Honey, tell me what's wrong," he pleaded.

She was sobbing so hard, she couldn't get the words out to tell him of her latest miseries.

"You stay right where you are," he ordered gruffly. "I'm on my way over."

His words were followed by a sharp click as he hung up the phone.

Laurel lay her head down on the kitchen table and sobbed as Cecile quietly let herself in the back door.

"Good heavens, Laurel." Her sister walked over to the sink and wet a paper towel with cold water. "The world isn't coming to an end. Pull yourself together."

"*My* world is!"

Cecile lifted her face and wiped the tears away gently, as she would a small child's. "No, your world isn't coming to an end. You've just had a bad day."

Laurel took the paper towel and blew her nose as she tried to regain control of her shattered emotions. "Sometimes I don't know what gets into me," she hiccuped. "Sometimes I want to tell the whole world to go to hell and leave me alone!"

"And you think you're alone in that feeling?" Cecile walked over to the refrigerator and took out a pitcher of lemonade.

Moments later she set a frosty glass filled with

the icy liquid in front of Laurel and took the chair opposite her. "I can sympathize with you in regard to the damages you've been plagued with, but I cannot understand why you're treating Dan this way. He's been like a member of this family for years, and all of a sudden you're treating him like *he's* the one responsible for all your troubles."

"Maybe he is!"

Cecile looked shocked. "Why, Laurel Henderson. You should be ashamed of yourself."

"Since when did you get so palsy-walsy with Dan?" Laurel snapped.

A soft flush rose in Cecile cheeks. "I've always liked Dan."

"Before you left for California, you never knew he was alive," Laurel challenged. "Why the big switch now?"

She hated herself for thinking what she was thinking right now . . . that there was more to Cecile and Dan's story than met the eye, but she couldn't help it. Not with the evidence against them continuing to mount daily.

Cecile sighed and crossed her hands on the table in front of her. "Why don't you sell this farm, Laurel? You're not happy running it. Now that Dad's gone, there's no reason to stay on here and be miserable. You need to start a new life, one filled with the music you love . . . and maybe a man in your life. You've buried yourself away for so many years, you have no idea what you're missing."

"Don't you think I realize that?" she hurled at

her sister. "But what am I supposed to do? I'm in debt up to my eyeballs, and if I sold right now, I'd barely come out with the clothes on my back. And what about you?, Where would you go? You haven't got a job, no means of support . . ."

"You can't be worrying about me," Cecile intervened. "I'll go out and get a job."

Laurel looked at her sister wryly. "Doing what?"

"I don't know. Waiting tables, clerking in some department store . . . I'll find something."

"You're not trained for anything other than being an actress," Laurel pointed out.

"Then maybe I'll find myself a good man and settle down," Cecile bargained. "Who knows what I'll do. The important thing is for *you* to get on with your life before you turn old and bitter before your time. I've had my chance and I blew it. Now it's your turn. Sell the farm, Laurel. Just as soon as humanly possible."

Find herself a good man and settle down?

Laurel felt a strange sense of unease. Who would Cecile go after? Dan or Clay? The thought that it might be Clay sent her into fits all of a sudden.

"What about Dan? Do I turn him out in the cold? If I sold the farm right now, I couldn't promise him that the new owner wouldn't replace him as foreman immediately."

"Then sell the farm to Dan," Cecile prompted softly. "He loves it, Laurel. Surely you're aware of that."

Laurel shook her head slowly. "Dan doesn't have the money to buy this farm, Cecile."

"He might be able to scrape enough together," she reasoned. "I know he has a little savings—not much—but you said yourself that you're going to have to take a tremendous loss on the business. What better person to lose to than someone who's almost family?"

Laurel's heart literally ached. Her own sister trying to sell her down the river.

Sure, sell the farm to Dan, and when Laurel limped away with her meager pittance, the two of them could build the farm back into the thriving and profitable business that it could be.

"Why are you looking at me that way?" Cecile peered at Laurel anxiously.

"Is there something going on between you and Dan?"

Cecile's mouth gaped open. "What . . . ?"

"You heard me. I saw the two of you walking together the other night, and you didn't come in until late—"

"Are you spying on me now?"

"No, of course not. I just happened to be looking out the window, and I saw you and Dan."

"So?"

"So. Is there something going on you haven't told me about?"

Cecile's eyes narrowed. "Would it upset you if there was?"

Laurel looked uneasy. "No."

It wouldn't bother her at all if Dan and Cecile

174

had a romantic interest in each other, but it *did* upset her to think they were conspiring to take her farm away from her.

"I just thought you might be interested in Clay, since you were going out with him tonight." Laurel was mortified to hear her voice turn so resentful all of a sudden.

"Who says I can't enjoy both of them?"

"Well, I don't think you should play one against the other."

"I don't plan to." Cecile looked at her coolly. "Why the sudden interest in Clay Kerwin? Not very long ago you two were fighting like cats and dogs over turkey feathers."

"Because," Laurel continued absently, "Dan was hurt very deeply once when he lost his wife and child, and I don't think you ought to go out with Clay if you're really interested in Dan. Dan deserves the loyalty of a good woman," she added in a protective voice.

"Laurel. I understood you to say on many occasions that you didn't care for Dan in a serious way. Are you saying you do now?"

"Heavens, no. I've told both you and him that," she denied.

"What about Clay?"

"Clay. Oh, uh, Clay . . . no, I'm not seriously interested in Clay . . . I don't think."

"Then why should it concern you if I take an innocent moonlight walk with one and go to a harmless German festival with the other?" Cecile pressed.

Before Laurel could tell her, Clay's patrol car

swung in the drive, and he braked to a hurried halt.

Seconds later he was knocking at the back door.

"Have you called Clay about the feed bins already?" Cecile looked surprised as she got up to let the sheriff in.

"Good morning, Clay."

"Hi, Cecile. Is Laurel here?"

Cecile motioned toward the table as Clay removed his hat and stepped past her.

"Are you all right?" Clay suddenly towered over Laurel's small frame as she blew her nose once more and glanced up at him sheepishly.

"Yes. Now I am."

"I'm going to take Dan a glass of lemonade," Cecile murmured. "Would you like one, Clay?"

"Thanks, but I don't have time." Clay gave her a polite smile. "I'm due to give a safety speech over at the school in fifteen minutes."

"Well, if you'll excuse me." Cecile glanced at Laurel, then back to Clay. "I'll see you tonight?"

Laurel cringed at Cecile's reference to her date with Clay that night. It was as plain as the nose on her face that she wasn't going to be satisfied with just Dan.

She wanted Clay too!

"Yeah. I'll pick you up early. I have to be on duty by six."

"I'll be ready." Cecile picked up the glass of lemonade she had just poured. "Laurel, I'll be outside in the barn if you need me."

"Now, what in the world was all that boo-hooing about a few minutes ago?" Clay reached for a kitchen chair and straddled his large frame over it comfortably. "I thought you were dying."

"Oh, Clay. I'm tempted to pick up that phone, call Paige Moyers, and tell him he can have this darn farm if he'll come and take it off my hands!"

"Paige? What would he want with this farm?"

"His grandparents used to own it," she explained, and dabbed at her eyes. "He's offered to pay me a very fair price for it, and before I let Dan and Cecile run me out of business, by golly, I'll sell it to him!"

"Paige Moyers's grandparents used to own this farm?" Clay frowned and looked at her skeptically. "Are you certain of that?"

"That's what he told me the other day."

"That's strange. This is the first I've ever heard of it."

"I was a little surprised myself, but I suppose he knows what he's talking about, even though he is terribly forgetful lately."

"Yeah, I'd noticed that too. It's probably his age. How old is he now?"

"I'm not sure . . . somewhere in his sixties."

"And he's offered you a fair price for the farm?"

"Actually, more than fair under the circumstances." She laughed ironically. "You know how Paige hates to let go of his money."

"Yes, I do. That's what surprises me about this whole situation."

"Well, regardless, he wants it, and I'm within an inch of letting him have it," she warned.

"I gather something new has happened?"

Laurel proceeded to tell him about the ruined feeders and the disturbing morning events, including her recent round of words with Dan.

Clay shook his head. "I sure hate to think Dan and Cecile are in on this. I'm going over to the Rowden farm to have a talk with Jake and Eddy as soon as I make my speech. Even though they don't own a truck, they could get their hands on one."

"But Cecile said she saw them running across the field last night," Laurel felt obligated to mention again. "Of course, she might have told me that just to throw us off track."

Clay rubbed his eyes wearily. "I doubt it, but I'll check it out."

Suddenly Laurel felt ashamed for going to pieces the way she had on the phone earlier, causing him to have to make an extra trip out here.

"I'm sorry you had to come way out here," she apologized.

Clay glanced up and met her solemn gaze. "Hey, I don't mind. It gave me the unexpected pleasure of seeing you again."

Laurel was horrified to feel her cheeks growing warm.

"Our date still on for tomorrow night?" he queried lightly.

"Yes, certainly."

"Everything all set?"

The color in her cheeks mounted at his intimate inquiry.

"Uh . . . no, not yet," she admitted. "But it will be by tomorrow evening."

Clay's blue eyes held hers captive. "Good. I'm looking forward to it."

His deep voice sent shivers rippling up her spine as he reached over and absently traced the contours of her tearstained face.

"You still going over to Freistatt tonight with Dan?"

"Oh, dear. I'm afraid I couldn't talk him into taking me to a dogfight right now," she confessed. "I guess I'll have to go alone."

"Alone? I don't think so." Clay's face grew openly possessive. "There's a lot of partyin' that goes on at one of these shindigs, and I don't want you going by yourself."

"My goodness, Clay." Laurel laughed. "Just because we're going to have an affair doesn't mean you have to feel responsible for me," she protested.

"Look, I can't help it, but I do. Okay?"

"But I go every year," she rationalized. "Sometimes I have a date, and sometimes I don't."

"I don't want you there by yourself, Laurel. There's a lot of unattached men running around, and you know how they get when they've had too much beer. It's usually innocent fun, but I won't have time to keep an eye on you."

"I know. You'll be too busy watching Cecile," she grumbled.

His grin was a very wicked one. "Oh, I plan on watching all the pretty girls . . . that's my job."

179

"And I hope you fall off your horse," she volleyed crossly.

The volunteer deputies all rode horses during the festival. They helped to park the cars in an open field and patroled the large, fun-loving crowd.

"If I do, it'll be because I'm trying to keep an eye on you and do my job at the same time. So, why don't you make it easier on both of us and don't go alone."

"But I want to go," she pleaded.

"I'll talk to Dan on my way out and have him take you."

"He won't do it. It will probably take us all day to replace the feeders, and he'll use the excuse that he's too tired to go because he's still mad at me."

"He'll go. I'll explain how you lost your temper and you're sorry. You can call in some of the neighborhood boys you use part-time to help you and Dan get the feeders back in operation. That way you'll have the job done in half the time."

"I suppose you're right." That did make more sense than for Dan and her to struggle to get the job done by themselves. "But I'm still not convinced my accusations are unjust," she said with a sniff.

"That remains to be seen, but until we find out something definite, we're not going to run around taking cheap pot shots at the poor man. Okay?"

Laurel cast her eyes down to the floor. "Well, I *do* want to go tonight."

"Then let me handle it." Clay leaned over and kissed her affectionately. "You just hustle on down to the drugstore before the day's over and get us set up for tomorrow night. I'll take care of everything else."

She grinned shyly. "I will."

He gave her a sexy wink and reached in his pocket to toss her a piece of bubble gum. "Save me a polka tonight?"

"Sure."

She sighed as she unwrapped the gum and popped it in her mouth. Clay disappeared out the back door in search of Dan.

Chewing thoughtfully for a moment, she positioned the gum on her tongue and began to blow carefully.

Seconds later she had a gigantic bubble almost covering her entire face.

Wiggling her eyebrows Groucho–Marx fashion, she recalled Clay's parting words: "Save me a polka?"

Well, he could be sure of that. She would indeed save him one.

Maybe even ten.

CHAPTER TEN

The little town of Freistatt, Missouri, was about an hour and a half drive from the farm. Not far from the Arkansas border, it had a population of one hundred and fifteen people. But every year around the end of August, close to ten thousand southwest Missourians who claimed some German heritage descended upon the small town for a weekend of folk music, polkas, and all the bratwurst, kraut, and German potato salad they could eat. Known as the Ernte-Fest in German, Harvest Festival in English, a roaring time was usually had by all.

The long, exhausting day was finally drawing to a close as Laurel glanced over at the man behind the wheel of her pickup. "I appreciate your taking me tonight, Dan. I know you must be tired out after the day you've just put in."

"It's my pleasure," he returned politely, keeping his eyes on the road.

"I don't want you to feel as if you had to bring me," she insisted. "I told Clay I was perfectly capable of making the trip myself."

"Neither Clay nor I thought that was wise."

They rode along without speaking for a moment as they listened to a popular country music song playing on the car stereo.

"I'm surprised they were able to refill the feed bins on such short notice," Laurel commented a few minutes later.

"Yeah. I explained the situation to the feed store manager, and he was nice enough to send a truck right on out."

"That was nice."

Another few minutes of silence passed.

"The weatherman says there's a chance of showers by morning," Laurel noted hopefully.

"Let's hope it materializes this time."

When the silence stretched to an unbearable length this time, Laurel decided she was going to have to apologize to Dan. It wasn't like him to be so aloof to her.

"Dan."

"Yes?"

"I'm sorry."

Dan's eyes never left the winding road as he waited for her to continue.

"I know I've upset you lately with some of my fits of temper, but I want you to know that they were just that. I realize you have as much interest in the well-being of the farm as I do. Surely you can understand what pressure I've been under and forgive me for my outbursts," she finished softly.

"I realize you're having a hard time right now," he said calmly, "but you have to realize that I find your accusations very hard to swallow.

I've been with you for a long time now, Laurel, and I think, if nothing else, I should have at least earned your full trust."

"I've never actually accused you of anything," she murmured.

"Not with so many words, but those green eyes of yours have sure had me before the firing squad a couple of times lately."

Her head drooped in shame. He was right. She may not have actually voiced her suspicions, but she had sure thought them zealously.

"Well, anyway. I want you to know I'm truly sorry for being so nasty, and from now on I won't be so hasty with my allegations."

For the first time in a very long time Dan smiled at her.

"Apology accepted. Now, what do you say we forget all about the farm and just let our hair down tonight and have a good time. I think we both need to let off a little steam."

Laurel's smile was radiant as she gratefully returned his smile. "I think that sounds wonderful."

The remainder of the ride was pleasant and relaxing. They talked of everything except the farm and the depressing lack of rain. Before she knew it, they were turning into the large field where men on horseback were directing traffic.

"Do you see Clay anywhere?" she asked, peering at the various riders dressed in their attractive blue uniforms. The car bumped along the dusty field, throwing up a cloud of dust as they were waved on by the riders' large red flashlights.

"Not yet, but I'm sure he's around somewhere."

Moments later Laurel rolled down the truck window and called out to a rider just coming out from behind a row of cars.

"Hey, Sheriff!"

Clay turned. When he saw Laurel waving at him, he tipped his hat and grinned back at her.

They were too far away from each other to make conversation, but somehow her mood improved one hundred percent when she saw him sitting so handsomely astride a large chestnut horse.

"You two seemed to be getting along better lately," Dan observed as he pulled the car into a parking place and killed the engine.

Laurel murmured something unintelligible as she hurriedly shot out her side of the car. At the moment she didn't want to get into any in-depth conversation with Dan concerning her much-improved relationship with Clay Kerwin.

The crowds were as large as they had been predicted to be, Dan and Laurel realized as they walked the half-mile or so to the festival area.

"Wonder where Cecile is?" Dan mused out loud as his eyes searched the crowd for the blond-haired beauty.

"Probably in the Bier Garten." Laurel laughed. "Want to check there first?"

He glanced at Laurel, his cheeks red. "Oh, I was just wondering out loud. She's here with Clay tonight, anyway."

"Clay looks like he's going to be tied up for a while," Laurel noted. "Let's see if we can find Cecile and keep her company until he's through."

The look of gratitude on Dan's face was all Laurel needed to push him in the direction of the Bier Garten.

They made their way through the thronging crowd to the roped-off area where they could purchase beer for the evening. Raising hands of friendly greetings to almost everyone they passed, they filed through the deputies who were standing guard at the gate to check ID.

The five-piece German band was tuning up in the background as Laurel and Dan walked around looking for Cecile.

But it was an impish Cecile who found them first.

"Boo!" Cecile crept up behind Dan's back and playfully punched him in the ribs. He jumped, then turned to greet her with a broad smile. "Hi! Hey! We've been looking for you," Dan exclaimed, his voice filled with relief that they had found her so quickly.

The smile she gave him made Dan's search well worthwhile. "I've been looking for you too."

"We just got here," he assured her, his eyes drinking in all of her.

For a moment it seemed to Laurel that they'd both forgotten all about her. They looked at each other for so long, she was finally forced to clear her throat and remind them.

"Yoo hoo . . . remember me?"

Cecile glanced at her sister. "Oh, Laurel. Hi."

"Hi."

"Uh ... you want a beer or something, Laurel?" Dan stammered uneasily.

It was certainly amazing how quickly his admiration had turned from one sister to the other, Laurel thought wryly.

"No, thank you, Dan." She peered at them solemnly, trying to keep a straight face. "Listen, would you mind keeping Cecile company while I sort of roam around? I've seen several people here I want to visit with, and I'd hate to keep you standing around while I socialize."

"No, of course not," he said, beaming. "You go right ahead and enjoy yourself. Cecile and I will find something to do."

"Gee, thanks."

She walked away grumbling irritably under her breath that he didn't have to be *that* obliging. She forced herself to recall Clay's words about their innocence of any wrongdoing until they were proven guilty ... but it was hard.

A few minutes later she had forgotten all about Dan and Cecile as she chatted happily away with some old school friends she bumped into.

"The band is beginning to play again!" One of the men in the group took Laurel's arm, and they all headed for the pavilion.

The tuba player was oom-pah-pah, oom-pah-pah, oom-pah-pah-ing away as they broke off in couples and started in a fast polka around the concrete floor.

A brisk, refreshing breeze had sprung up, making the evening perfect for such a gathering.

Laughter rang out as happy couples danced by each other and called out friendly greetings.

The man Laurel was dancing with was a giant compared to her modest height, and they looked like Mutt and Jeff careening around the floor.

"I swear, Milt, you grow taller every time I see you," Laurel shouted above the din of the music. "When are you ever going to reach your full height?"

Milt Brownleigh had been in her graduating class, and at that time he had been tall, but now . . .

"Don't know. My wife says she's going to have to start carrying a stepladder around with her when she wants to hug my neck!"

Her eyes continued to make an occasional search he suddenly lifted her up off her feet and waltzed her around the floor in playful theatrics.

For the next hour the beer flowed as readily as the marvelous polka music. Laurel refused to sit out of the fun until she was almost ready to drop.

Her eyes contined to make an occasional search of the crowd for Clay, but so far she had been unable to locate him.

She frowned when she spotted Beatrice Mosely dancing with a fellow at the far end of the pavilion dressed in a blue uniform the same as Clay's. When she was able to assure herself a few minutes later that it wasn't Clay, but another volunteer, she felt much better.

She was beginning to think of Clay as hers and hers alone, and it both irritated and pleased her at the same time.

"All right, folks!" The leader of the band held up his hand for attention. "We're going to have a change of pace now. Grab your partner and get ready, 'cause we're going to do the bird dance!"

A roaring cheer from the crowd went up as the bandleader announced one of the favorite dances of the evening.

From the corner of her eye Laurel noticed Paige Moyers standing on the sidelines with a big grin on his face as he watched the couples pairing off.

Turning to catch his eye, she held out her hand and motioned for him to come be her partner.

He blushed and waved her suggestion away with embarrassment.

Deciding that Paige needed a little excitement in his life, she marched over and took him by the hand to drag him out on the dance floor.

"Oh, no, Laurel! I can't do the bird dance," he begged. "I'm too old for this!"

"Sure you can! If all these people can make fools out of themselves, we can, too, Paige!"

The music started, and the fun began. After a few introductory bars of the music the bandleader called out, "Now let's all try our bills." He placed his hand on his nose and wiggled his five fingers energetically.

The crowd responded in like manner as the

tuba oom-pah-pah, oom-pah-pah-ed in a moderate tempo.

"Now our wings!" Arms obediently folded and hands were placed in armpits, flapping wildly as the "human" birds followed instructions.

"Now our tails!"

Chortles from the sidelines and dance floor broke out as the dancers placed their hands on their bottoms in imitation of a tail and exaggeratedly swayed their hips to the beat of the music.

"Now let's put it all together!" The dancers began to move around the floor, trying to keep time with the music and be "birds" all at the same time as the beat of the music began to pick up.

"Now our bills!" Wiggle! Wiggle!

"Now our wings!" Flap! Flap!

"Now our tails!" Sway! Sway!

Around the floor they moved amid peals of giggles. Laurel was almost in tears, she was laughing so hard at Paige's deep concentration on his actions.

"Isn't this fun?" she shouted, brushing at her eyes.

He glanced up, grinned, and flapped his wings halfheartedly. "Not really!"

The beat of the music was increasing regularly now, until the tempo reached *prestissimo*.

"Now our bills!" Wiggle! Wiggle!

"Now our wings!" Flap! Flap!

"Now our tails!" Sway! Sway!

The dancers were energetically going through

the motions to the beat of the polka music, trying their best to keep up with the fast music.

A young boy came sailing by Laurel and Paige, doing a solo version of the dance and entertaining the crowd with his hilarious antics.

Suddenly the music shifted back to a moderate tempo once more, allowing the dancers a moment to catch their breaths.

"Hear you had a little trouble out by your place last night," Paige said, puffing.

"Yes, someone tipped over all my feed bins," she confided.

He whistled under his breath. "Must have been quite another hefty loss."

"Yes, it was."

The feeders cost a whole lot, and then she had to have them all refilled. The loss would be staggering when the bills were tallied.

He shook his head sadly. "Oh, Laurel. I wish you would let me help you. You're losing ground every day. Won't you let me buy the farm and put you out of your misery?"

"That's sweet of you, Paige, but I couldn't do you an injustice like that. Until we find out who's causing all this trouble, it would only mean you pouring good money down the drain. You know I'm losing money faster than I'm making it."

"I know, but I can't stand to see you upset like this."

She patted his dear old head in affection. "You're a good friend, Paige, and I love you for being concerned about me. I'll admit that if you had been around this morning, I would have *given* you the farm, but now I'm feeling a little better about things."

"Well, you know I'm always there to help you," he chided. "You're like a daughter to me, Laurel. By the way, how is your mother doing lately? I haven't seen her in some time."

Laurel patted him on the shoulder patiently. "Paige, my mother died giving birth to me. Did you forget again?"

This was the second time he had brought up Laurel's mother in the past few weeks.

"Oh . . . my goodness." He looked properly embarrassed. "I don't know what's wrong with me lately. Of course, Julia's gone. How silly of me!"

"That's all right. . . ."

Laurel felt a peck on her shoulder. She turned around, her face breaking into a wide grin as Clay stood before her, solemnly wiggling his hand on his nose.

"I believe this is our dance, Madame Bird?"

"I'd be honored," she returned with a demure flap of her wings.

Clay glanced at Paige. "Do you mind?"

"Mind! I'd *pay* you to take this feathered beauty off my hands!"

They both laughed as they watched him walk over to the bleachers and slump down wearily.

"Now, let's all get those bills a workin' again!" The announcer shouted once more.

Laurel and Clay faced each other and bent

192

over, jauntily wiggling their hands in front of their noses.

Their eyes locked with each other, and he sent her an intimate greeting that she couldn't fail to receive.

"Hi, honey. I've been looking all over for you," he said warmly.

"I've been looking for you too," she confessed, loving the way he was calling her "honey" with increasing regularity.

Her heart was doing flip-flops at the way his eyes were lazily inspecting the curved neckline of her blouse and the gentle swell of her breast as she leaned toward him and went through the playful motions.

"Now our wings!"

They circled each other, flapping their arms and smiling at each other. It occurred to Laurel that Clay had turned this silly little dance into a sexy waltz between them. Even though they were not touching each other in any way, she knew that in his mind he was holding her in those strong, powerful arms that looked so darn sexy beneath his blue uniform.

"You been having fun?"

"I am now," she returned coyly.

"Now the tails!"

His grin deepened wickedly as he bumped his bottom with hers as he circled.

Laurel turned and swung her jean-clad fanny in Clay's direction, more than willing to play this titillating game with him.

His eyes darkened to a smoky blue as he

193

paused and watched every delicious movement she was making as she placed her hand on her bottom and swayed her "tail" enticingly for his benefit alone.

She had never been so brazen in all her life, but it sent her blood racing to see the look of desire flare brightly in his eyes. It gave her a sudden power she was hesitant to turn loose.

A knowing smile spread across his handsome features as he followed her lead, his eyes never leaving her hypnotizing movements.

"Little bird, if we were alone, I don't think you would be doing that," he breathed softly as he leaned over and brushed his mouth against hers. "Not unless you were prepared to pay the consequences."

"I am prepared," she bantered. "But, alas, our date isn't until tomorrow night."

"You come with me and I'll show you just how fast we can change those plans," he coaxed in a sexy whisper against her ear.

"You're not supposed to be bothering the bird by whispering in her ear," she chided.

"The bird isn't supposed to be bothering me, either," he warned as she continued to sway her slender hips in motion to the music. "And she's going to embarrass us both right off this dance floor if she doesn't stop."

Thankfully the beat began to pick up once more until the dancers were racing through the motions. Minutes later they collapsed against each other, still laughing when the dance finally ended.

She lay against his chest in a heap and gasped for breath. "Wasn't that fun?"

"A barrel of laughs. Now come on. I want to continue this somewhere in private for a moment."

Laurel let him lead her through the crowd as she tried to catch her breath. They were stopped a couple of times by friends who offered to buy them a drink, but Clay waved them away and continued pulling her along after him.

"Where are we going?" she asked as they rounded a corner and ducked behind a parked automobile.

"We're going somewhere I can do this."

He stopped and pulled her possessively to his taut chest, his mouth coming down roughly on hers.

She sighed and wrapped her arms around his neck, surging closer to the comfort of his now familiar body. For several long moments they stood kissing, devouring each other's mouths hungrily.

When Clay finally broke away, he buried his face in her hair and rubbed his hand affectionately over her rounded bottom.

"I hope to heaven you didn't dance with anyone else out there tonight like you just danced with me. I thought once or twice I was going to have to arrest you for indecent exposure."

"I wasn't exposing anything," she denied, letting her hands explore the width of his arms she had admired so shamefully all evening.

His mouth closed over hers once more, and

his tongue parted her lips and searched for its mate.

All of a sudden it just seemed so right for her to be here in his arms. Their affair had gotten off to a shaky start, but that hadn't seemed to dampen his ardor in the least. She was immensely relieved that he seemed to want her so badly.

It was a long time before they were able to pull themselves away from each other this time. When they did, they both were humming inside like two powerful, high-voltage wires.

"Tomorrow night seems an awful long time away, don't you think?" he asked in a husky whisper.

"Terribly long," she agreed.

"I don't know why you didn't let me break the date with Cecile tonight and bring you," he complained. "That way we could have slipped away from here early and . . . spent some time alone together."

"Have you even seen Cecile tonight?"

"No, I haven't," he confessed. "I've been busy until a few minutes ago. I suppose I should look her up and ask for a dance."

"Well, don't worry. She's in good hands," Laurel noted. "Dan has been with her ever since we got here."

"To be honest, I'm glad Dan's keeping her busy. At least this way we can spend a little time together."

"Shame on you, but that's exactly how I feel too," she said, grinning.

Laurel leaned back and peered at him expectantly. "Did you see the way those two were looking at each other? Now, you try to tell me something fishy isn't going on!"

"I'll admit there seems to be an obvious attraction between them, but I don't see what's so strange about that. She's a good-looking woman and he's a single man."

"I know, but it seems strange to me that Cecile wouldn't let me know she's interested in Dan. I tried my best to get her to admit she was when we talked this morning, but she refused. If she has nothing to hide, why doesn't she just come right out and say, 'I think I'm falling in love with Dan'? She certainly hasn't ever hesitated to tell me about her new loves in the past."

"I don't know. Maybe she thinks you're in love with Dan."

Laurel shook her head thoughtfully. "I've told her I wasn't."

"Well, I'll get to the bottom of all your troubles. Just hold on." He kissed her again, lingeringly. "Are you feeling better about life this evening than you were when I last saw you?"

"Yes. I'm sorry I went bananas."

"I was worried about you," he confessed.

"I was worried about myself," she said with a laugh, "but I got over it."

"Did you get the feeders replaced?"

"Yes, thanks to Dan and the neighborhood boys, everything is back in order." She sighed and lay her head on his chest. "For today, at least."

His hands rubbed her back in silent assurance. "Hang in there, sweetheart."

"I will. At least until I can sell the farm."

Clay's hands ceased their movement. "I don't like to think about you selling, Laurel."

"There are days when I don't, either," she confessed. "I know I'll miss it."

"Then don't sell."

"I don't think I could go to school and handle the farm at the same time, Clay," she confessed in a small voice.

"Is it really that important that you go back to school?"

"To me, yes."

"And you want to move away from here?"

Laurel had to think a minute before she could truthfully answer him.

Her feelings for him were growing every day. If he had asked her that same question three weeks ago, maybe even a week ago, she would have had no difficulty in answering him. But now . . . Did she want to move away from Clay Kerwin?

"I don't know. Paige just offered to buy the farm again a few minutes ago, and it was a big temptation to tell him yes."

"He offered to buy it again? I can't figure him out."

"Oh, he's just being a friend. He says I'm like the daughter he never had, and when he heard about the latest trouble with the feed bins, he felt sorry for me again."

"How did he know about the feed bins? Did you tell him?"

"No, I didn't say anything. I thought maybe he had talked to you or Dan earlier."

His hands started their slow exploration of her back once more. "What would prevent you from selling the farm to Paige but staying here while you went to school?" he wondered softly.

"Well, for one thing, the university is a long way off," she reasoned.

"You could rent a small place near the campus and come home every weekend," he pointed out.

"I don't know, Clay. It isn't just furthering my music I'm concerned about. I may not have enough money to even live after the estate is settled and I'm able to sell the farm. My dad had some staggering medical bills, and with my recent business losses, I'll probably be flat broke. I want to try my wings at life," she admitted. "And I don't want anything—or anyone—to keep me from doing that. Ever since I can remember, I've had obligations to someone or something. Just once in my life I want to be footloose and fancy-free."

"Then that's what we'll work on," he said gently. "Maybe in time you'll come to realize that being footloose and fancy-free isn't all that it's cracked up to be. As for a taste of life, well, you'll have a head start on that after tomorrow night." His eyes caressed her intimately.

"Oh, yes, I'm ready for tomorrow night," she

said, sobering. "I made it to the drugstore just before I came this evening. We're all set."

His hand trembled just slightly as he touched the tip of her nose. "Good. I couldn't talk you into starting this affair a little early . . . say, after I brought Cecile home this evening?"

"No, I don't think so. She would think something was suspicious if I left the house again."

They kissed another long kiss.

"Did I tell you how handsome you look in your uniform?" she asked a few minutes later.

"No, but I think you'd probably like me better without it," he teased, and nipped at her ear.

"That's entirely possible." She gasped as his exploring mouth sent cold shivers racing through her. "But . . . the uniform . . . does great things . . . to me . . . too . . ."

"You like it?"

"When we first drove up and I saw you there, you know what went through my mind?" Her hands trailed down the front of his shirt and unbuttoned the top two buttons.

"No, tell me."

"With your Indian heritage . . . you know, your dark skin and dark hair and the way you have of lifting your head and looking so proud and solemn at times . . . well, I could almost picture you a hundred and twenty-five years ago sitting on your horse in nothing but a breechcloth, long, black hair blowing in the wind, your blue eyes looking out across a vast prairie land."

"Nothing but a breechcloth and blue eyes?" He grinned. "You have a real vivid imagination. Did I have any scalps hanging from my saddle horn?"

"Oh, no, you're not that sort of Indian," she assured him. "You're one of the nice ones, although I'll admit I can't for the life of me think of a tribe that chewed bubble gum."

"No? You ever hear of the Sioux Indian?"

"Sure. Is that what you are?"

"No. I'm a Chew Indian. We were close cousins, though."

She slapped him across the chest irritably. "You idiot!"

His face sobered somewhat. "Does my being Indian bother you, Laurel?"

Her eyes softened as she leaned down and pressed her lips to his bare chest. "That doesn't bother me, Clay Kerwin. But everything else about you is beginning to."

"Do you remember how an Indian used to capture the woman he wanted and take her back to camp as his, and she didn't have a thing to say about it?" he murmured, then caught his breath as her tongue traced patterns along the base of his throat.

"Yes."

"What would you think if I did that to you?"

"You wouldn't."

"Why not?"

"Because, that was then and this is now. You know, women's liberation." She giggled and kissed him briefly. "Spoiled everything, didn't it?"

She was pulled back roughly against him, and for a moment she was back a hundred and twenty-five years being kissed with the fervor of a savage . . . and it was wonderful.

"I *am* going to do that one of these days, Laurel Henderson," he warned with a smothered groan. "Be prepared."

Laurel looked at him innocently and grinned impishly at his poor choice of words.

"I'm tryin', I'm tryin'!"

CHAPTER ELEVEN

"Buck, what do you know about Dan Colburn?"

Clay sat in his office the next morning, blowing bubbles and idly tossing darts at the reelection poster of Tucker Mason, the sheriff of the neighboring county.

Buck glanced up from the paperwork he was doing and thought for a moment.

"Not a whole lot. Seems like he's a pretty nice guy. Lost his wife and child several years ago, and he sort of went off the deep end for a while, but I think that's all behind him now. Why?"

"No particular reason." Clay squinted his eyes and took careful aim at a spot directly between Tucker's two shifty eyes and let the dart fly. It whizzed through the air with perfect accuracy and landed exactly on target. "I've been racking my brain all morning to recall what little I know about the man."

"He's a quiet sort. No one knows a whole lot about him. Moved here with his wife when they first got married. She had some family living around here somewhere," Buck said.

"They still here?"

"No, seems to me like I heard they moved away shortly after their daughter died."

Another dart went sailing through the air and pinned one of Tucker's ears flat to the wall.

"You thinkin' Dan might have somethin' to do with the trouble out at the Henderson place?" Buck prompted.

Growing tired of his game, Clay lobbed the last dart at the poster and pushed back from his desk. He ambled over to the window, stretching his large frame and yawned.

"Not really. Just thinkin' in general," he replied absently. "What about Cecile Henderson?"

"What about her?" Buck got up from his chair and walked over to the coffee urn.

"Think she's on the up-and-up?"

"Well, now, that depends. Never have cared for Cecile like I have her sister, Laurel, but then that's just my personal preference."

"What don't you like about her?" Clay persisted.

Buck dumped several packages of sugar in his cup, then filled it with black coffee. "Can't put my finger on it," he confessed. "I suppose I never have trusted them showbiz people."

Clay chuckled. "You think she'd be low-down enough to try to run her own sister out of business in order to get her hands on the farm?"

"Can't see why she would," Buck pondered thoughtfully. "That farm is barely scratching out a livin'. Ain't good for nothin' except running a few head of cattle or raisin' them turkeys."

"Yeah, that's what I keep telling myself," Clay murmured. "Yet . . . there's something going on I can't quite put my finger on." He ran his hands through his hair irritably. "What would Dan and Cecile want with an old farm that's losing money every day?"

"Dan and Cecile?" Buck glanced at Clay ambiguously.

"Laurel thinks there's something going on between her sister and her foreman."

Buck let out a low whistle. "Is that a fact?"

"I can't argue with her that Dan and Cecile are obviously attracted to each other, but for the life of me I can't come up with any viable motive for them to run Laurel out of business. Dan has put a lot of years in building up that farm, and a man just doesn't tear down what he's poured his sweat and blood into. No, that theory just won't hold water, Buck."

"I heard Cecile was cut out of her father's will," Buck speculated. "Maybe it has something to do with that. Greed can make a person do strange things. If Dan and Cecile are involved with each other, maybe they want to get Laurel out of the picture and have the farm and money all to themselves."

"What money?"

"Well, Sam surely left a goodly little amount to Laurel," Buck reasoned.

"No, he didn't. Laurel says that with her father's medical bills and the several large business losses she's had lately, she's going to be almost broke when the estate is settled. But even if he had left the farm financially secure, Cecile and Dan couldn't get their hands on any of it unless something happened to Laurel . . ." His voice paused in mid-sentence and his face turned pale. "Damn, I hadn't thought of that."

His heart raced as it suddenly occurred to him that Laurel's very life could be in grave danger. This recent vandalism could be leading to higher stakes if the culprit failed to scare her out of business.

"You don't think this matter is *that* serious, do you?" Buck peered at him anxiously. "It's not been that big of a thing . . . some power lines cut, a dog turned loose in the grow-out house, the feed bins . . ."

"It seems to be getting bigger each time," Clay pointed out, his expression strained and worried now. "I've got to do something."

Buck took a sip of his coffee and shook his head. "Hadn't thought about the possibility of it turning into anything serious." He glanced up at Clay's worried countenance. "This goes deeper than just your job, doesn't it?"

Buck had worked with Clay since Clay came on the force as a deputy several years ago. He had seen the look of desire flare in his eyes when Laurel Henderson walked by the office window. He had even teased him about the pretty auburn-haired girl, telling Clay how he looked at her like a kid peering into a candy store. Clay would only grin and shrug off his lighthearted banter. But Buck couldn't be fooled. Clay Kerwin was in love with Laurel Henderson. Always had been.

Clay was watching out the window now as he mulled over Buck's words. Yes, it went much deeper than his job, and he was tired of trying to tell himself it didn't. He still loved Laurel as much today as he had when he was just a kid. If anything happened to her, he would never live through it. It was his responsibility to protect her and he would. Come hell or high water, no one was going to touch one hair on her head as long as he was still breathing.

"Kind of sweet on the lady, aren't you?" Buck said.

And for the first time in all the years Buck had teased him about Laurel, Clay decided to be honest.

"Yeah. I'd marry her tomorrow if she'd have me."

Buck grinned. "What's the matter? The old Kerwin charm slipping?"

Clay shrugged.

"Come on, boy. It's not like you not to be able to bring a woman around to your way of thinking," he teased.

"Oh, I'll get her," Clay acknowledged. "I'm just going to have to give her enough rope to hang herself."

Buck was still chuckling as he walked back over to his desk and reseated himself. "This ought to be fun to watch."

Clay sobered once again as his thoughts went

back to the problem that was always on his mind.

"Buck, I want you to see what you can find out about Paige Moyers for me."

"Paige Moyers?" Buck glanced up, looking confused.

"Yeah, for some reason he's got it in his head that he wants Laurel's farm. I want to know why."

"He's getting senile, Clay. Surely you've noticed that."

"Yeah, I have, but just do a little checking around for me. Let me know what you come up with."

They both glanced up as the door opened and the object of Clay's affections stepped through the doorway.

"Hi, guys!" Laurel smiled at the sheriff and his deputy.

Clay's face brightened as he walked over to greet her. "Hi, honey. This is an unexpected surprise. What brings you down here?"

Their eyes met, and they both fought to conceal their happiness at seeing each other.

"Oh, I just tried my luck at making candy this morning, and I thought you might enjoy some," she explained, drinking in the sight of him in his crisply ironed uniform.

"Candy?" He peered at the large plate she held in her hand. "You didn't need to go to all that trouble. What kind is it?"

He leaned closer, and a puzzled look came

over his face as he tried to make out the garish-looking green lumps on the dish.

"What's your favorite kind?" she coaxed.

"I don't know ... fudge?" he guessed. If it was fudge, something was terribly wrong.

"Nope. Guess again."

He searched his brain for the right flavor. He liked peanut brittle, but if *that* was peanut brittle, he couldn't imagine what she had done to it.

"I don't know," he admitted in a guilty voice. "Maybe that white stuff my mom used to make around Christmas time. Divinity?"

"That's it!"

His shoulders slumped with relief. The candy wasn't white, so it was a sheer miracle he had hit on the right recipe.

"Gooseberry divinity!"

A shudder rippled through his large frame for just a brief moment before he was able to shake it off and compose himself. "Gooseberry divinity." He smiled sickly. "Mmmm ... my favorite."

"I have to admit I don't know how well it turned out," she warned. "I've never made that flavor before ... but here." She hurriedly unwrapped the plate and offered him a piece. "Try one."

Clay cast a helpless look in Buck's direction. The deputy had his face buried in his coffee cup trying to control a fit of laughter.

Clay gingerly picked up one of the greenish wads. "Looks delicious," he lied.

"Thanks." She smiled proudly. It was nice to

be able to have a man around to ply with his favorite foods.

"Well?" She grinned at him in encouragement. "Go ahead and take a bite."

"I don't know, Laurel. I just had a big breakfast a little while ago. Maybe I should save it for an afternoon treat. . . ."

Laurel's face grew stormy. Sure. He had been stuffing his face with Beatrice Mosely's biscuits, and now he was too full to eat the candy she had slaved over all morning.

"Well, it's up to you," she said in a frosty tone, walking over to offer a smirking Buck a piece of her confection. "But if I were you, I'd stop going over to the café every morning and gorging myself on biscuits. It's beginning to show."

Clay eyes shot down anxiously to his flat belly. "It does?"

The smirk dropped off his deputy's face as he sat up straighter and somberly tried to make his selection from the pieces of candy lying on the plate.

"I'm sure my candy isn't half as tempting as Bea's biscuits," she muttered under her breath. "Buck! That's the smallest piece on the plate," she chided. "Here, take two." She dumped two fat drops on his desk and walked off.

Seeing how disappointed she was that he hadn't dived into the candy energetically, and taking into account her none too discreet hints about Bea's biscuits, Clay hastened to pop the tart candy in his mouth.

There was immediate, excruciating pain as his saliva glands rebelled and threatened to lock up on him permanently. His eyes started watering as he stubbornly willed his jaws to chew and his face to remain expressionless.

"Good." He grinned at her and took another bite.

"You like it?" She watched him expectantly.

He nodded, because by now he couldn't have spoken if his life depended on it. Glancing over to see how Buck was faring, he had to turn away quickly.

His deputy was trying to chew his way through the gummy concoction, looking very much like an old cow trying to chew her cud.

Managing to swallow the last bite, Clay prayed she wouldn't insist on *him* eating two pieces.

There was absolutely nothing that could improve the flavor of this candy, with the exception of a garbage disposal. But even with Clay's limited knowledge of candy making, he thought at least four more cups of sugar might have made a difference.

"Well"—he dusted his sticky hands off and stood up—"you've outdone yourself this time, honey. That was the best gooseberry divinity I have ever eaten. Bar none. Don't you think so, Buck?"

Buck looked rather comatose as he struggled to swallow the last bite of his candy. He nodded weakly. "It shore was!"

"Are you guys only going to eat one piece?"

Laurel asked, her voice sounding hurt and disappointed.

"Hey." Clay raised his hands in defense of their actions. "We want to have something to look forward to this afternoon."

"Well, I suppose it would taste better later on, especially if you've just eaten," she relented.

Clay leaned over and gave her a peck on the tip of her nose. "Thanks for thinking of me. I really do appreciate it, and I promise I'll enjoy every bite this afternoon."

And he would if it killed him, which it might.

Buck quickly pushed back from his desk and reached for his hat. "Think I'll mosey on over to the drugstore," he said.

Clay shot him a grateful look. "Yeah. Why don't you, Buck. I can handle things around here."

Buck's grin was knowing. "Kinda thought you could. Be back in fifteen minutes or so."

Before the door had closed on the deputy's back, Clay had Laurel in his arms.

"Come here, you little dickens," he said with a growl. "Let me say good morning to you in the proper way."

"Why, Sheriff Kerwin!" She batted her eyes coyly, regaining her former good disposition in spite of Beatrice Mosely's biscuits. "I thought you'd never ask."

They went into each other's arms and started the day the only way a day should be started.

"Mmmm . . . you taste like gooseberries," she murmured a few moments later, then paused and nibbled at her lips thoughtfully. "Clay, did the candy have enough sugar in it?" She peered at him expectantly.

Since he had no desire to get into a discussion about her candy, he pulled her back in his arms and smothered her with kisses amid her laughs of protest.

They contented themselves with outright necking for the next five minutes before Clay remembered that he was in an office where anyone could walk in at any time.

"I hate to be the one who breaks this up," he said as she traced the outline of his lips with her tongue, "but we're in a public office. . . ."

"I know. I really should be going," she conceded in a wistful voice. "I promised Dan I would be right back."

Once more their mouths met in a lingering kiss.

"I'll be by for you tonight around six," Clay whispered.

"Six? I thought you were coming at seven."

"I can't wait that long," he confessed, nibbling at her lips as they talked.

"Clay, I've been thinking. People are going to start talking. You know this town. Already we've been seen together more than we should. I'll come to you tonight."

"I don't care if people talk," he argued.

He wouldn't care if the whole world shouted from the rooftops that he was seeing Laurel Henderson.

"I know, but I don't want all the busybodies

to know what I'm doing," she said, fretting. "And I have a feeling Doc Odell is going to be watching every move I make."

"You're sure we're all set to go?"

"I'm positive. Don't be such a worrywart," she said, teasing him.

"Now be sure, Laurel, because I can stop and pick up something—"

"No, Clay. I'm the one who suggested this affair, and I'm the one who will see that it's carried out in a dignified and orderly fashion."

He pulled her up tighter against his growing desire."I just want to make sure nothing will go wrong tonight," he murmured in a suggestive voice. "I'm beginning to hum like a buzz saw."

"It won't," she promised, growing weak from the feel of his body pressed tightly against hers and the thought of unknown delights yet to come. "I have the proper precautions bought and ready to go."

Clay kept her pressed close to him. "I thought maybe we'd stay at home tonight"—he kissed her eyes—"cook some steaks"—he kissed her nose—"maybe swim for a little while. . . ." His mouth captured hers coaxingly as she leaned against him and returned the kiss.

"Like you did with Bea on your birthday?" she demanded, and could have kicked herself.

"Yeah, only we'll do things a little different this time. I'll end up taking you to bed. Bea ended up doing the dishes."

"Really?"

Their eyes met.

"Would I lie about a thing like that?"

"Yes."

"Well, I'm not." He smacked her on the bottom and finally released her from his tight embrace. "Wear the skimpiest bathing suit you can find," he ordered. "And now, go home before we both get into trouble."

"I can't. I have to go shopping for a bathing suit."

"I thought you had to go home and work."

"I'll call Dan. There isn't that much going on today, and besides, Cecile is there if he needs anything."

The mention of her sister's name reminded Clay of a question he had meant to ask her. "Honey, did you tell me you'd made out a new will and left Cecile as the soul beneficiary?"

"Yes. Paige is drawing up the papers now. Why?"

"No reason. I'm just trying to piece a puzzle together."

Laurel gazed at him solemnly. "Has something new developed in your investigation?"

"No, nothing new." His arms moved around her protectively. "I wish I could stick you in my shirt pocket where I could keep my eye on you all the time," he said softly.

They stood wrapped in each other's arms until they heard the front door open, signaling Buck's return.

"I'll see you tonight," Clay promised as Laurel left the office.

*   *   *

On the drive over to Clay's house that evening, Laurel mulled over in her mind what was about to take place.

She would be entering a new phase in her life—a welcome one for her—but nevertheless, she would never be the same Laurel again once this night was through.

Is this what she really wanted?

The answer was a muddled yes . . . and no.

Yes, she wanted to have an affair with Clay Kerwin. But by falling in love with him, she would be destroying every opportunity for the freedom she had wanted for so many years. At this point she wasn't ready to settle back into the same old trap she had been in all her life . . . was she?

There was a great big world out there just waiting for Laurel Henderson. A world where she could quench her thirst for music and knowledge and have a little fun, instead of beating her brains out raising turkeys.

No, she could not permit her growing feelings for Clay to interfere with her future plans.

When the farm was back on its feet—or maybe even before then—she would start her new life. Meanwhile she would have the affair with Clay, knowing that he could remain uninvolved. Clay had been a bachelor far too long to take this project seriously. Every woman in town had tried to catch him. So Laurel didn't have to worry about his getting hurt when the time came for them to break off the relationship . . . if it ever got started.

She patted her little drugstore sack for reassurance. And tonight would be the night!

When she pulled in the drive, Clay was waiting there to greet her, the two basset hounds at his feet.

"Your home is quite lovely," Laurel praised as they went around back to the pool area. "I meant to tell you that when I was out here the other day."

"You've never been inside, have you?"

"No."

He leaned over and kissed her, his masculine after-shave making her senses tingle. "You will. I plan on giving you a personal tour, ending with the master bedroom."

"Umm . . . sounds interesting," she murmured shyly.

"I think you'll find it a lot more than just interesting," he promised. "You need somewhere to change into your suit?"

"No, I already have it on."

She unfastened her tomato-red sun dress and let it drop around her ankles.

Clay stood back to survey her turquoise, two-piece swimsuit, which, she had to admit, was the skimpiest she could find.

The sudden darkening of his eyes was all she needed to assure her that her choice had been the right one.

"They actually make you pay money for that

scrap of material?" he asked, his voice breaking with huskiness.

"Do they ever! Cost me an arm and a turkey." She grinned. "Like it?"

"It was worth every penny you had to pay," he complimented, letting his eyes wander freely over all her curves. She had a slim, wild beauty that made him want to take her in his arms that very moment and consummate their relationship.

"I never realized you were so . . . small." His eyes surveyed her petite, almost delicate frame with longing.

She frowned. "Is that a compliment or disappointment I hear in your voice?"

"Honey, I can assure you, everything you'll hear from my lips concerning you will be a compliment," he vowed affectionately.

She saw the male predator look in his eye and sidestepped his forthcoming kiss. She ducked under his arm and ran to the edge of the pool.

"Last one in's a turkey feather!"

Clay peeled off his shirt and dived in the water beside her.

"Are you chicken?" he asked when he surfaced, referring to her hasty entrance into the pool.

"Maybe."

"You didn't give me time to examine your suit properly," he accused.

"I think you saw enough," she chided, splashing water in his face playfully.

"No, I didn't," he denied. "I didn't see nearly enough."

"You'll have your opportunity," she encouraged.

"I have a great idea. Why don't you take it off and throw it up there on the ground. Then we can both admire it while we float around out here," he reasoned with a boyish grin.

"Ummm . . . maybe later. Someone might walk up on us."

"No one will walk up on us. I live out in the country, remember?"

"I walked up on you and Bea," she reminded.

"Oh, yeah, but she had her suit on," he was quick to point out. "And if I hear one more word about Bea, I am going to turn you over my knee and paddle that tempting bottom of yours."

Laurel's face sobered. "Clay, do you see her anymore? I mean . . ."

"No, and if it will make you happy, I'll even quit eating breakfast over at the café," he bargained.

"But you love her biscuits."

Clay shrugged. "They're passable, but I think I'll start eating cold cereal."

They swam for the next few minutes, splashing and dunking each other until Laurel pleaded for mercy.

"Don't dunk me again," she said, gurgling as they both went under for the fourth time.

Under water, Clay pulled her flush against him, and they kissed until she thought her lungs would burst.

When they surfaced a few moments later, she

was gasping for breath and clinging to his neck for support.

"Are you trying to drown me?"

"Yeah."

"Well, stop it."

"No, I like you when you're helpless," he teased. Wrapping his arms around her waist, Clay kissed her as his hands explored the gentle curves of her waist and hips.

His touch turned her to pure liquid as she murmured his name and caressed his mouth lightly with hers.

The sexual tension hummed between them and once again made him think of high-voltage wires. When he was with her, it was electric, powerful, almost frightening in its intensity.

She could feel his need for her building into explosive proportions as one long kiss followed another.

His touch was tender and loving as he finally summoned up the nerve to slide his fingers under the top of her suit and touch her intimately.

Their eyes met and held.

Gazing at her with adoration so painfully evident, he sighed and closed his eyes for a brief moment to savor the feel of her breasts held tightly in his hands.

To touch her in this way, to hear her moan and move her softness against his rigidity, to hear her whisper his name in longing, to feel her fingers tightening in his hair as he gently stroked her breasts . . .

"I want to see all of you," he whispered.

In unison they moved to the edge of the pool, and Clay lifted her out of the water like a small baby.

Seconds later he joined her at the edge of the pool, his lips unable to cease their exploration of her.

Laurel had not expected events to move along quite so rapidly, but it seemed they both had a hungry need for each other that begged to be satisfied.

Her hands ran over the corded muscles of his chest as he unsnapped her top and feasted his eyes on her loveliness.

Crushing her to him, he pulled her on top of him, his hands running over her bare back in sweet exploration.

"I want you, Laurel, I want all of you," he murmured in a strangled voice as he devoured her mouth over and over.

"Oh, Clay, I'm so afraid I'm falling in love with you."

"Would that be so horrible?" The blue of his eyes grew dark with longing as they gazed at each other.

"I . . . don't know. I thought this would be a simple affair with no strings attached. . . ."

"Nothing in life is simple, with no strings attached. Don't fight this thing between us, Laurel. You're mine . . . you always have been and you always will be, if I have to wait until I'm a hundred years old to make you see that we belong together."

"But what about my life . . . ?"

"But what about mine?"

They kissed again, and he peeled the rest of her bathing suit off and tossed it in the water.

"Let's talk about this later, huh?"

"Should I get ready . . . ?"

She hated to sound stupid, but she didn't have the slightest idea of what to do next.

"I'm ready if you are," he coaxed.

"Are we going in the house?"

His mouth found hers again as he whispered, "That would take too much time. We're alone here. Don't worry."

"Can you reach my beach bag?"

Sitting up on his elbow, he jerked the bag off the table and handed it to her.

Reaching inside, she extracted an aerosol can and a plastic vial.

"This is supposed to be ninety-some-odd percent effective," she assured as she looked the apparatus over.

"Great." At this point Clay really wasn't interested in statistics. "I'm sure it will do fine. Just hurry."

"All right. Now, let me see." She carefully unfolded the instructions and proceeded to read. "Insert end of vial into can. . . ."

"Couldn't you have read the instructions earlier?" he demanded.

"I meant to, but I forgot. Hand me a towel, will you? I'm getting the paper wet."

Clay grumbled something and snatched the towel off the back of a lawn chair.

Wiping her hands, she picked up the can and vial and studied it for a moment. "You know anything about this stuff?"

"Me?"

"Yes. Have you ever used it?"

"How would I use it?" he asked blandly.

"Well, I didn't mean you in general. I meant, have you had any experience with this—"

"No, and can you hustle a little bit?" he pleaded, feeling his ardor diminishing rapidly.

"Oh, sure. This should be easy."

She went back to perusing the instructions.

"Oh, ye gads! Clay. This is sick. Do they honestly expect me to get into this position?"

Clay looked over her shoulder at the detailed picture and let out a low whistle. "Surely not."

"Well, I'm not going to."

"It probably doesn't make any difference how you do it, Laurel. Just hurry up."

"All right. Don't rush me or I might make a mistake."

Clay let out a long breath and ran his hands through his hair. "You're making me nervous. I wish I had a piece of bubble gum."

"You don't need one. I think I have it clear in my mind. Now, all you do is insert end of can into vial . . ."

She pursed her lips in deep concentration, and there were a few moments of complete silence.

"Something's wrong," she announced.

"Oh, hell. What is it this time?"

"I don't know. I can't get anything to come out," she confessed meekly.

He snatched the can out of her hand and shook it violently.

"Don't do that! It might blow up!"

"There's a better chance I'll blow up faster," he grunted. "Hand me that vial."

More silence followed as he tried his luck at extracting some of the can's contents.

Only a sticky dribble of white oozed out for all his trouble as he finally lost his temper and pitched both vial and can over the fence.

"Clay!"

"Face it, Laurel. It's curtains again tonight."

"You shouldn't have thrown it away," she scolded. "I could have taken it back to the drugstore and gotten my money back."

He groaned and rolled over, burying his face in the towel.

"Don't be so upset." She consoled him smugly. "I'm not quite as stupid as you think. It so happens I brought a backup system."

One hopeful blue eye came out from hiding. "You did?"

"Yes. I really couldn't decide if we would like that gook, so I bought an additional product to try next time."

"You did!" He came out from beneath the towel, new hope shining in his eyes now. "Where is it?"

"On the dash of my truck. I didn't have room in my bag. . . ."

"Stay where you are. I'll go get it."

He sprang to his feet and was off like a scalded cat.

She had to congratulate herself on her foresight. They would have been in a fine pickle right about now if she hadn't been so efficient. And Clay would not have been nearly so happy.

But Clay's face was anything but happy when he rounded the corner a few minutes later with a white package in his hand. He dropped it glumly at her feet.

"What's wrong?"

"You know how hot it is in that truck right now?"

"No. How hot?"

"Hot enough to fry an egg on the dash . . . or, more to the point, hot enough to melt your 'backup supplies' back to their original form."

Laurel frowned and opened her sack. The feminine suppository was indeed nothing but pure liquid now. She glanced up at Clay helplessly.

"Oh, gad. What do we do now? Did you happen to get . . ."

He shook his head, his stern face growing sterner. "You distinctly told me not to. You said *you* would take care of everything."

"Maybe the drugstore or market . . ."

"No way, Laurel. You know everything but the filling station shuts up in this town by six o'clock."

Her face brightened. "Does the filling station have one of those little machines—"

"No!"

"Well, you don't have to get mad!" she snapped back. "None of this was my fault!"

Clay was so frustrated by now, he was fit to be tied.

"Do you know what this is doing to me?" he accused angrily. "I'm going nuts!"

Laurel reached for her sun dress and hurriedly slipped it back on.

"Well, it hasn't exactly been a barrel of fun for me either, Clay Kerwin."

"Where do you think you're going?"

"Home."

"No, you're not. We haven't even eaten yet."

"I'm not hungry."

She snatched up her beach bag and marched angrily around to the truck. If that ungrateful so-and-so wanted to put all the blame on her, then he could go fly a kite.

"Laurel! You march right back here," Clay ordered helplessly.

"Leave me alone, Clay," she warned as she hopped in the truck and started the engine. "Our 'affair' was obviously a mistake. It seems I haven't got the brains and you haven't got the patience to get it right." Tears welled up in her eyes.

"Honey . . . look, don't go off mad like this," he pleaded, reaching out to touch her cheek in gentle persuasion. "Laurel, honey, I'm not mad. . . ."

But she was in no mood to listen.

Seconds later he was watching the disappearing tailgate of her truck bump down his drive.

Clay slammed his hand against the tree and cursed under his breath as the two bassetts looked up at him in silent commiseration.

CHAPTER TWELVE

The phone was ringing off the hook when Laurel walked in the door. She knew without a doubt who it was.

Picking up the receiver, she sniffed and dabbed at her eyes once more. "Clay, don't even try to talk to me right now. I'm mixed up."

"You can't just walk out on me like that," he said impatiently. "I've been worried to death about you. Where have you been? I've been trying to call you for the last hour."

He fired questions at her in rapid-fire order, causing her tears to flow once more.

"I went for a drive."

"Where?"

"Down by the river."

There was a pregnant silence on the other end of the line. "Our river?"

"Yes . . . our river." She had felt a need for total privacy and had instinctively headed for the place where she and Clay had spent so many happy hours.

"Honey, I know you're upset about tonight,

but it was just one of those things," he coaxed in a soft voice. "Next time I'll take care of—"

"No. I don't think there's going to be a next time," she interrupted.

Clay heaved a tired sigh. "Don't say that."

"I mean it, Clay I can't believe I'm so inept that I can't even have a simple love affair properly," she said, sobbing.

"Laurel, don't start crying again," he pleaded helplessly.

"I can't help it. This night is the most humiliating night of my life."

"Look, I'm not upset about it, so why should you be?"

"You're just saying that to make me feel better," she accused. "How many other women in your life have been so totally klutzy?"

Well, she had him on that one.

"There is only one woman in my life at the moment, and she is far from being klutzy," he said, trying to console her. "Why don't I come over and pick her up and take her out for a bite to eat and discuss this thing rationally? Surely we are adult enough to come up with a workable solution to this."

Laurel sank down on the stool next to the phone and continued to mop her eyes dry. His tenderness was making this so much harder. Why didn't he tell her what a poor excuse for a woman she was and be honest about what he was thinking?

"I don't think so, Clay. I think we should put this affair on hold for a while."

"Why?"

"Because . . . because all of a sudden I don't know what I want or where I'm going or what I want to do," she confessed with another sob. "My life is nothing but one big uncertainty, and I just can't seem to handle it anymore."

Clay's heart sank. He had been afraid something like this would happen.

"Are you going to put it on hold, or are you trying to tell me you want to find another man to have the affair with?" he asked in a tight voice.

"Of course not. I wouldn't subject myself to this humiliation with anyone else," she snapped.

"Why don't you just go back to the doctor and get the pill?" he reasoned. "That should take care of matters."

"It would delay the affair by at least a month," she shot back.

"So? I'm not going anywhere."

"Clay! Aren't you getting just a little uptight after all these . . . delays?"

"I'm sure I'll survive," he said. "I just want you, Laurel—" His voice broke before he gained control of his battered emotions and spoke again. "Let's just forget about tonight and start all over again."

"Right now I don't want even to think about it," she muttered.

"Then don't . . . but don't make any final decisions about anything," he coaxed. "We'll let things ride for a while. I know you have a lot of things on your mind."

"I do, Clay. I really do," she accepted gratefully. "If I can just get this batch of turkeys to the market and out of my hair, then maybe I'll get back to normal."

"How much longer will it be before they go to market?"

"Another couple of weeks."

"Then what?"

"I don't know. That's what I'm going to have to decide. If I'm lucky and the price of turkeys stays up, I just might be able to break even. If I do, then I'm thinking of selling the farm to Paige."

"Laurel, please don't do anything rash," Clay urged uneasily.

"Rash? Paige has offered me more for the farm than I could dream of getting anywhere else. He is well aware of the problems I've been having, so I could sell it to him with a clean conscience. Why would that be rash?"

"Because at the moment you don't know what you want to do. You said so yourself. Right now you're so confused, I'm scared to death you're going to make a big mistake, honey."

"Well, it certainly wouldn't be my first," she wearily admitted.

"What you need is something to eat and a good night's rest," he told her gently. "You'll see things differently in the morning light."

"I suppose you're right. I'll eat a sandwich, then take a hot bath and go to bed."

"Sounds good. And Laurel . . ."

"Yes?"

"I won't push you on this affair bit, but I want you to know that I want it . . . more than I've ever wanted anything in my whole life."

Clay's voice had turned almost shy. He held his breath and waited for her answer.

"I just don't know, Clay." She sounded weary.

She wanted to promise him anything he wanted. Oh, how she longed to tell him that before this was all over, they would spend at least one night in each other's arms, but she couldn't.

She had no idea what course her life was going to take once she got the turkeys to market.

"I've never asked for any promises," Clay reminded her. "All I want to do is make love to you, Laurel Henderson. I have from the first day I set eyes on you."

Tears swam in her eyes at his heartfelt confession.

"I . . . I have to go, Clay."

"Good night, sweetheart."

Laurel replaced the phone and had herself a good long cry.

What in the world was she going to do about Clay Kerwin?

The next couple of weeks crept by. The heat kept up, and so did the persistent acts of sabotage. Someone tampered with the propane supply, causing the heat to be shut off in the brooder house for an entire twenty-four hours.

Luckily the poults were far enough along, so they didn't need the extra heat or it would have resulted in another disaster.

But the following week Laurel was not as lucky. This time the power lines were cut leading into one of the grow-out houses in the very heat of the afternoon.

With no electricity the cooling fans were unable to operate and, as a result, at least four hundred more birds were lost due to suffocation.

And so it went, day after day, until Laurel thought at times that she would lose her mind.

The only consolation in those grim days was Clay's daily phone calls to let her know he was working as hard as he could on solving her problem.

That still didn't change the fact that, in Laurel's opinion, Clay was getting absolutely nowhere. But it helped to know that she wasn't in this thing alone anymore.

The subject of their personal relationship was carefully avoided.

The second bright spot was the slowly improving relationship between her and Cecile. Cecile was beginning to lose some of her aloofness toward the farm and, most of all, toward Laurel.

Laurel couldn't put her finger on what was causing the change, but she instinctively knew it was connected with Dan.

Cecile had been disappearing for long periods of time in the evening, and Laurel felt sure that she was with her foreman.

Even Dan's disposition had improved lately, and she could hear him happily whistling under his breath as he went about his work.

But if Cecile and Dan's dispositions had sweetened, Laurel's had curdled.

"Damn!"

Laurel irritably threw the pencil down on the table and glared at the paper soundly. "I'm sorry, Paige. What do I do? Scribble over my name and start all over again?"

She had been sitting at the breakfast table one morning with Cecile and Paige Moyers, trying to sign more of the endless estate papers that kept coming her way. Now she had made a royal mess of her signature.

Paige patiently picked up the papers and stuffed them back in his briefcase. "No, I'll have Tess retype them, and you can sign them later on." He snapped the case shut and looked at her benignly. "I'm worried about you, Laurel. You've lost weight and you look pale. Are you eating properly?"

"No, she isn't," Cecile supplied. "She hasn't eaten enough to keep a mouse alive the last two weeks."

"It's too hot to eat," Laurel dismissed irritably.

"That never stopped you before," her sister noted.

"It's the pressure of this farm that's getting you down," Paige scolded. "Now, I know it's none of my business but I don't think Sam would want me to stand by and watch your health being damaged over this nonsense."

"I'm all right, Paige, or at least I will be if I can just hold out long enough to get the turkeys to market by tomorrow morning."

"Oh? You're going to load tonight?"

"Yes. It's a little early, but the processing plant can take us a few days ahead of schedule. I called and explained to them the problems I've been having, and we're going to take a shot at getting the birds in and weighed out before anything else happens."

"You'll be running the risk of having a smaller weigh-out," he warned with a worried shake of his head.

"I know, but at best I'm only going to break even with this flock. I'll have to take the chance."

"Well, I certainly hope that once you get those birds to market, you'll reconsider my offer to buy the farm," he reprimanded sharply.

Laurel glanced up at him, surprised to hear the impatience in his voice now.

"I *have* been thinking about it, Paige, and after the birds are sold—"

"Laurel," Cecile broke in. "Would you like another piece of toast?"

Laurel surveyed her half-eaten piece lying on her plate. "No, thanks. I'm not going to finish the piece I have."

"What were you about to say, dear?" Paige sat up closer on the end of his chair and waited for Laurel to finish her remarks.

"I was saying . . ."

"More coffee?" Cecile stood over her, the coffeepot poised in her hand.

"Uh . . . no." Laurel looked up at her sister. It wasn't like Cecile to be quite so . . . hostessy.

Paige wasn't at all pleased with the constant interruptions. "Please, Cecile. I'd like to hear what Laurel was about to say."

Never one to be shy about expressing her opinions, Cecile put one protective hand on her sister's shoulder and said coolly, "Laurel isn't herself lately, Paige. I don't think she's ready to make any permanent decision about selling the farm."

"Cecile!" Laurel glanced at her sister in protest.

"I mean it, Laurel. I think you need more time to think about this."

"I've had several weeks," she challenged. "Several long, miserable weeks."

Cecile sat down in her chair and took hold of both of Laurel's hands. "I know it's been rough on you, but after we get the turkeys to market in the morning, we'll start all over again. We still have the brooder house full of young poults."

"Start all over again?" Laurel asked incredulously. "And lose thousands more dollars!"

"It won't be that way this time," Cecile promised. "You'll see. Things are going to straighten out this time."

Paige glanced at her sharply. "How can you predict that? Laurel has had nothing but trouble for the last few months. No one has been able to catch the culprits, and they are out there waiting to sabotage any flock of new birds that Laurel brings in. How can you sit there and encourage your sister to bring more hardships on herself?"

"Because I love her and she's my sister," Cecile stated defiantly. "I don't want to see you pressure her into selling something she's worked her tail off for most of her life!"

"Cecile!" Laurel gasped at her rudeness to the family attorney.

Paige stiffened. "I'm sorry you feel that way, Cecile, but I fail to see why you've taken this sudden interest in your sister's welfare. After all, you didn't seem to care how the farm was handled when you took off for California a couple of years ago."

Laurel could scarcely believe her ears. She had never heard Paige or Cecile say one unkind word to each other, and all of a sudden they were at each other like cats and dogs.

"Maybe I've learned a few things since those days, Paige," Cecile said in a calm voice. "And one of the things I've learned is not to make hasty decisions."

"The decision is not yours to make," he pointed out in a tight voice. Suddenly he picked up his coffee cup and angrily flung it at the kitchen counter. The women watched in disbelief as the china shattered over the floor and the brown liquid ran down the front of the cabinets. "You have no right to say these things! No right at all!" Paige yelled. "Sam left the farm to Laurel, and she can do what she wants with it."

Both Laurel and Cecile were stunned at his irrational actions. Never had they seen him raise his voice in anger. Now he didn't even seem to notice what he was doing.

Reaching for Cecile's hand in a calming gesture, Laurel spoke quietly. "Paige, there is no reason for you to become so upset. Cecile was only expressing her opinion."

Paige looked at Laurel as if he just remembered she was there. "She's trying to interfere in your life, Laurel. I don't want to see that happen," he protested, his voice once more taking on a quiet fatherly tone.

"I'm sorry, Laurel, but I still think you would be making a mistake by selling the farm right now," Cecile repeated.

"Even to Dan?" Laurel tried to gauge her reaction to her unexpected challenge.

Cecile cast her eyes downward. "Even to Dan. If . . . if you'll keep the farm, I'll try to run it while you go back to school."

Laurel looked at her in disbelief. "Are you serious?"

This was growing more confusing by the moment.

"I've never been more serious in my life. I know you don't understand, but I think this is something we should talk over in private."

She cast a heated glance at Paige, who was sitting quietly and listening to the two sisters' conversation.

"Well, if you ladies will excuse me"—Paige reached for his briefcase and stood up abruptly—"I have work to be done."

Laurel could tell he was upset, and she made

an effort to appease him as she walked him to the back door. "I'm sorry about this, Paige, and I will give serious thought to your offer, but if Cecile is serious about staying here and running the farm . . ." She shrugged helplessly. "Well, I can't turn my back on her."

"I think it is a big mistake to let her talk you into keeping the farm," he confessed in a grave voice. "But the choice is yours."

"I'll call you in a few days," Laurel promised. "I should have an answer one way or the other by then."

Paige leaned over and gave her a fatherly kiss. "It's your welfare I'm concerned about. You know, it's a sad fact, but the people we love most in the world sometimes try to stab us in the back." He looked at her knowingly. "Try to bear that in mind when it comes time to think of your future. A person should have what's rightfully his. No one should stand in his way if he's earned it. . . ."

Did Paige know something Laurel didn't? Was it plain to him that Dan and Cecile were after her land, and he didn't want to hurt her by telling her so?

Closing the door, she turned to face Cecile. She wanted to find out what that heated exchange with Paige had been about, but she found the kitchen empty.

Well, she had the turkeys to worry about today. Tomorrow would be time enough to take on a new problem.

Loading turkeys for the processing plant was usually done at night, somewhere between the hours of ten P.M. and twelve midnight. A turkey grower doesn't question that practice, since a turkey is less flighty at that hour and is easier to handle.

Around eleven thirty that night, a fleet of trucks with wire cages welded to the beds pulled into the barnyard and stopped.

The loading crews had finally arrived.

It would take two full crews and almost all night to load the birds on the truck and drive them to the processing plant.

Once again time was of the essence.

Once loaded on the trucks, the turkeys would begin to dehydrate and lose poundage until they were unloaded at the processing plant.

The men had just begun their race against the clock when Laurel noted Clay's patrol car turning in the drive.

Her heart skipped a couple of beats as she watched him leave the car and start in her direction. She suddenly realized how much she had missed seeing him these last couple of weeks.

Oh, he had been by a couple of times to talk with Dan, and he never failed to look her up and share a few minutes of his day with her, but that had been all.

He smiled as he walked up and paused before her.

"Hi, Laurel Henderson."

"Hi, Clay Kerwin."

He took off his hat and ran his hand through his hair. "Thought I'd drop by and make sure there was no trouble tonight."

"Thank you. This is above and beyond the call of duty, isn't it?"

Clay shrugged his broad shoulders. "I had to go out to Ernestine and Howard's again, so I thought I'd stop by."

"Oh, dear. Are they at it again?"

Clay looked at her in disbelief. "Did they ever quit?"

Laurel giggled. "Was Ernestine chasing him with the broom again?"

"No, Howard finally had enough guts to take the broom away from her, but personally, I think that was a big mistake on his part."

"Why?"

"She was clobbering him with a sponge mop tonight," he said, grinning.

"Well, whatever the reason, I'm sure glad you're here."

"How glad?" he prompted softly.

For a moment their eyes met, and Laurel felt herself growing weak in the knees.

"Would you like to step around the side of the barn for a minute and find out?" Laurel asked quietly.

"Lead the way."

Laurel glanced around to see if anyone was watching, then ducked around the side of the building.

Moments later Clay followed.

"Please be gentle with me," he murmured,

love glowing in his eyes as he backed her up against the building and pressed against her. "It's been a long time."

It felt so wonderful to touch him again. Laurel closed her eyes and savored the delicious feeling.

"Oh, Clay. I think I've missed you."

"You damn well better have," he whispered huskily.

His mouth came down on hers, and he kissed her. His hand caressed her bottom and drew her closer to his taut thighs.

"You are going to have me in fine shape to help get turkeys to market," he grumbled when their mouths parted a few moments later.

"You don't have to help," she assured him. "Just your being here is enough for me."

"You mean that?"

She nodded. "I'm afraid I do. I've missed seeing you lately. Where have you been?"

She knew full well he had been giving her some badly needed breathing space, and she appreciated it, but enough was enough.

"I've been busy lately," he said evasively. He moved against her suggestively. "You really missed me, huh?"

"I really did," she admitted.

He was giving her another kiss when they heard Dan call her name.

"We'll have to continue this at another time," she cautioned, stealing one final kiss before she backed away from him.

"I'm going to hold you to that," he warned.

"I should hope so."

Dan was standing over by one of the escalator belts that was used to load the turkeys in the cages as they strolled over to meet him.

"You want me?"

"Yeah. Did you want me to go up to the house and bring down the cooler? The men are getting thirsty."

"No, I will. You're needed here." She glanced at Clay. "Want to go with me?"

"I'd love to, but I need to talk to Dan for a minute."

"Oh?" Her face fell. "Well, I'll be back in a minute."

Laurel left Clay talking to Dan as she hurried along the path to the house. Just then, from the corner of her eye she thought she saw something in the shadows. She stopped in her tracks.

Peering intently into the darkness, she watched for a few moments. When she could find nothing, she shrugged off the feeling of being watched and ran on into the house to get the cooler. She would never be so happy as when these turkeys were safely out of her care.

"I think we're about to break the case, Dan."

Clay and the foreman had stepped over into the shadows and stood talking as the loading proceeded.

"Is it who we talked about the other day?"

"Yeah, I think so." Clay shook his head sadly. "I don't want Laurel to know yet. If I'm right, the truth is going to hurt her."

Dan shook his head. "She's been through hell lately. She's going to take this hard."

Clay's eyes grew thoughtful. "Yeah, she is, but I plan on being here to help her through this."

Dan smiled. "I thought you might be."

Clay smiled at his new friend. "I hope I'm not cuttin' in on your territory, but I'm afraid that at this point you'd have to fight me for her."

"At one time I would have." Dan's face sobered. "But now—"

"But now you've noticed she's got a knockout of a blond-headed sister?"

Dan glanced up in surprise. "How did you know that?"

"Laurel told me weeks ago."

"Laurel knows about me and Cecile?"

"Sure. But she thinks you and her sister are the ones trying to take the farm away from her."

"Damn. I knew it. The only reason we haven't told Laurel about our relationship was because we wanted to be sure. That's the *only* reason."

"I never doubted that for a moment, and deep down I don't think she did, either. Anyway, it shouldn't be long before we can tell her the whole story."

"You expecting trouble tonight?"

"That's why I'm here. Buck's watching the road, and I thought I'd hang around here. We're dealing with a sick person, and I don't want to leave Laurel alone for a minute until I can get this case wrapped up."

"I hope you're wrong."

"I hope I am, too."

The loading proceeded without incident for the next couple of hours.

A brisk wind had sprung up, and the smell of rain was in the air. Distant claps of thunder could be heard as Laurel passed out the drinks and kept a wary eye on the approaching storm.

"*Now* it decides to rain," she complained as she handed Clay a cold drink. "I could swear someone has put a hex on me."

Clay laughed and started to try to console her when Dan let out a shrill whistle.

"Clay! Over here!"

Clay handed his can back to Laurel and took off in a dead run with Laurel following suit.

"What's wrong?"

Dan was standing before one of the trucks, his face grave. "Someone's cut the fuel line on this truck."

Laurel went pale. Hundreds of turkeys were already loaded on the truck, and they would smother in no time if they didn't get them to the Live Haul.

"Oh, no, Dan."

"I'm afraid that's not all," he said grimly.

Clay swore under his breath. "Go ahead."

"There's two more trucks down. They've had their tires slashed."

"How in the hell did they slip past us?" Clay asked incredulously.

He had been watching every move that was

made, and other than the loading crew, no one had set foot on this land all evening.

Laurel sagged against Clay weakly. This *was* the last straw.

She was bankrupt, and she might as well face it.

CHAPTER THIRTEEN

"All right. Let's not just stand here and talk about it. We have all those turkeys sitting here ready to smother to death. Let's get busy." Clay took off his hat and gun belt and quickly handed them to Laurel. "I'll fix the fuel line, Dan, if you'll take care of getting some new rubber on the trucks." He peeled his shirt off and pitched it to Laurel.

"It won't do any good," she cried, catching the shirt in her hand. "I'm ruined."

Clay turned around and pointed a stern finger at her. "Don't start crying, Laurel."

She stifled her sniffling immediately. "I'll try not to," she promised, but it was going to be all she could do to stop herself.

"We could always have the crew unload the turkeys again," Dan pointed out. "But that would take time and mean another financial blow to you."

"She's not going to do that," Clay decided firmly. "She may have to take some losses, but we're going to get those damn turkeys to market *tonight*, come hell or high water."

247

Clay took her hand and pulled her along with him as they started to run toward one of the vandalized trucks.

"Look around and tell me which of the crew members are missing," Clay shouted as they raced for their destination.

"Missing? What do you mean?" she called back, trying to keep up with his long-legged stride. "I think they're all here."

"No, they're not," Clay predicted grimly. "I'd bet my last dollar on it. Were there any new faces in the loading crew this time?"

"Well, sure, but that isn't unusual," she protested. "Drivers come and go."

Laurel started scanning the men loading the other trucks. In a few moments she had taken inventory and found two to be missing.

"There were two men who were loading out of number-three houses that aren't there anymore," she reported breathlessly.

"That figures. I knew it had to be one of the crew who's done this, because no one else has set foot on this farm since I got here."

"Maybe the men are just taking a break," she reasoned.

"No, they're *making* a break," he said, puffing. "But maybe Buck will stop them when they reach the road."

As they came upon the truck loaded with squawking turkeys, several of the men were standing by helplessly.

"Let's not just stand there," Clay barked. "Let's get this truck fixed."

The men went into action as Clay slid in under the large vehicle and began shouting muffled orders.

"Laurel, go find out if Dan keeps any spare parts in the storage barn."

Laurel turned and ran to find Dan. Minutes later she barreled back to the truck. Slumping against the fender, she held her side and tried to catch her breath as she spoke.

"He said, what kind of parts do you need?"

"Tell him if I'm lucky, I think I can repair the part that's on here, but if I can't, I'll need new rubber hose. And hurry!"

Laurel rolled her eyes and took off again in a dead run.

She came flying down the path a few minutes later carrying a box with various auto parts rattling around loudly inside.

Sweat was rolling in rivulets down her temples, and her clothes were matted against her from the high humidity. Meanwhile, streaks of sharp lightning arched toward the ground in the western sky as the storm front grew closer.

"He said this was all he had," she reported in a gasping wheeze. "He doesn't know if you can use anything in here or not." Laurel shoved the box under the truck for Clay's inspection.

There was no answer on his end. A few seconds later she dropped to her knees and peered under the vehicle to see what was going on.

Clay was busy trying to fix the severed fuel line, his mind totally engrossed in his work.

"Hey. Are you all right?"

He glanced out at her.

"Sure. Did Dan have any parts?"

Pushing the box farther under the truck, she repeated what Dan had told her.

For a minute she lay her head down on the dirty, rocky ground and watched him work.

His bronzed body was glistening with sweat now as he speeded up his efforts to repair the damage. Arm muscles rippled tautly as he jerked at a rubber hose and tore it loose. He swore as he surveyed the slashed hose and dug in his pocket for a knife.

Laurel's eyes closed for a moment, and she prayed as hard as she had ever prayed in her entire life. Not only for her selfish interests. They no longer mattered to Laurel. If she went broke, she went broke. The last few weeks had proved to her that it took more than money to make a person happy. Dan had worked so hard ... Clay was trying so hard ... Cecile had changed and was starting to be content with what life offered her. Please, God, I don't know how you'll do it, but *send me some help!*

"How's Dan coming on the tires?" Clay's voice broke into her thoughts.

"Not very well. He's trying to get hold of someone to bring new ones out here, but that will take time."

"What about your neighbors?"

Laurel hadn't thought of that. There was one neighbor down the road who owned a large dairy farm. He had trucks about the same size as the ones the turkeys were loaded on. Maybe he would have some spare tires to loan in an emergency.

A large clap of thunder shook the ground as Laurel jumped to her feet and ran toward the house. She was sure Hank Matthews wasn't going to like being woken up at this hour of the night, but she had no choice.

When she exited the house a few minutes later, her face looked brighter.

"Dan!"

Dan glanced in her direction as he and three other men were trying to jack one of the heavy trucks off the ground to remove the slashed rubber.

"Hank Matthews has some tires that will fit the truck."

"How many?"

"Only four, but that will help!"

They needed eight, but they would take anything they could get.

"Anything will help at this point," Dan shouted back. "I'll go get them." He took off in a run toward the farm pickup as the first big plops of rain hit the dusty ground.

The smell of rain pattering on the dry earth after such a long drought was heavenly to Laurel as she stood and took in long, deep breaths. And with the storm front came the wind. Cool, refreshing gusts of wind shook the metal buildings and bent the treetops nearly to the ground as the brunt of the storm bore down upon them.

Lawn chairs were picked up and wildly flung across the barnyard. Stray pieces of paper and twigs slammed against the vinyl siding of the farmhouse, and the air suddenly came alive with turkey feathers.

"Laurel, do you think we should go to the cellar?" Cecile came running from one of the grow-out houses. "One of the men heard on the truck's CB that tornado warnings are out."

"Oh, Cecile. He heard me!" her sister cried as she spread her arms wide and let the angry wind rip through her damp hair.

"*Who* heard you?" Cecile looked at her in exasperation.

"Don't you see what's happening?" Laurel cried. "Look at the turkeys, Cecile!"

Cecile turned and shielded her eyes against the flying dust and debris. "It looks to me like they're getting their tail ends blown off!"

"They are. But at least it's cooling them down!"

All of a sudden the sky opened up, and it literally poured. Large claps of thunder and almost simultaneous bolts of lightning cracked through the dark sky as the wind and rain picked up velocity.

One of the loaded trucks pulled up in front of where the two women were huddled, and the driver beeped the horn impatiently.

"I think that's Clay," Cecile shouted above the fury of the storm.

"He must be driving the truck to the Live Haul," Laurel shouted back. She dashed out into the blinding rain and ran for the truck.

Clay leaned over and opened the door for her as she jumped in the seat next to him.

"Isn't this marvelous!" she cried, leaning over to hug his neck with exhilaration.

Their mouths met in a quick kiss as he shifted into gear and started the truck rolling.

"Your guardian angel must be working overtime tonight," he said, grinning.

"I could hug his neck, too," she confessed happily. "Oh, Clay. I think we may make it after all."

"Never had any doubt," he said matter-of-factly as the truck, loaded to the brim with squawking, wet turkeys, wheeled out onto the country road.

Clay honked as they roared past the parked patrol car where Buck had the two missing crew men safely ensconced in the backseat.

"Hot dog!" Clay exclaimed. "Now we're finally beginning to get somewhere!"

He didn't want to let Laurel know, but this was the break he had been waiting for. With these two thugs in custody it wouldn't take long to get the name of who they were working for. Clay had a gut feeling what that name would be, but he needed concrete proof, and it looked like Buck had just gotten it for him.

"Were those the men who cut the tires and fuel line?"

"I'd say that's a safe bet," he murmured.

They sped toward the Live Haul, a cooling shed where the turkeys would be held until the processing plant was ready for them.

Laurel glanced over at Clay in the dim light of the dash and sighed. Now that the trucks were rolling again, she felt much better about the situation.

Scooting over close to him, she ran her hand over his damp skin and laid her head against his broad shoulder.

He smiled down at her quizzically.

"What do you think you're doing?"

Her fingers tiptoed up his sinewy rib cage. "Oh, I don't know. I just suddenly felt very . . . amorous toward you."

He looked at her in disbelief. "Boy, you can pick the darnedest times to make a pass at a guy," he marveled.

She smiled up at him and snuggled closer to his warm body. "You know I don't know how to do it right. Are you complaining?"

"Well, in a way, yes. Why don't you do this when I am not trying to haul a truckload of hot turkeys in a blinding rainstorm?" he suggested.

"I've done this before," she reminded, letting her hand gently caress his flat stomach. "Just because *you* never followed through with your part . . ." she bantered.

He shot her a warning look. "I'd be careful if I were you." He removed her roving hand and placed it firmly back in her lap. "The only reason I didn't follow through with my part was out of consideration to you," he stressed. "And I want to warn you right here and now; I won't be that nice about it again."

"Oh, good!"

He shook his head tolerantly. "You're pretty feisty tonight."

"I believe there's another word for it."

"If you want to do something to turn me on, why don't you show me your little 'bird tail'?" he challenged.

"You like that?" She sat up on her knees, placed her hand on her bottom, and wiggled playfully, the way she had the night they'd danced together at the Ernte-Fest.

He put his hand on his nose and made a bill, wiggling it in her direction. "I love it."

Leaning over to him, she murmured something in his ear that made his eyes grow dark and slumberous.

"What do you think?" She grinned.

"I think you'd better run for your life once we get these turkeys to market," he warned as her hand found its way back over to torment him.

"Clay."

"I'm not teasing you, Laurel. You'd better stop it. You don't realize that you're dealing with a desperate man right about now."

"Clay." She leaned over and kissed the center of his chest as he groaned and shifted around restlessly.

"What?"

"Will you stay all night with me?"

He chuckled. "I thought I was."

It was getting close to two A.M., and they still had many hours before the last turkey was hauled.

"No, I mean, will you stay with me in the morning when we finish our work?"

Clay's eyes grew tender as he heard the sincerity in her voice.

He knew she was hesitant . . . or just plain didn't know how to ask him for what she really wanted.

"I can't stay for very long, honey. I'll have to go to the office, but I'll stay with you for a while."

"You don't think I'm shameful?" she murmured guiltily.

"Yeah. I think you're shameful for waiting two whole weeks before you ask me to have another affair with you," he teased lightly.

"Another? We never did start the first one," she protested.

"Honey"—his eyes grew serious—"when we do get it started, it's going to be well worth the wait."

Their mouths touched and mingled sweetly.

"Think so, huh?"

"No doubt about it. But at the rate we're going, the affair is going to come after the marriage," he joked.

Laurel sat up and looked at him. "Who said we were getting married?"

"Well"—he kept his eyes straight on the road ahead of him—"I would marry you, you know. I keep hoping you'll pop the question."

She looked aghast. "You think I would be that gutsy?"

He let out a loud whoop. "The woman doesn't blink an eye when she's asking me to have an affair with her, but she chokes up when I suggest that she might propose marriage. That's rich."

"But marriage . . . that's so permanent, Clay."

Her face sobered at the thought. If she married Clay, she would be right back in the same old groove she had been in all her life.

No freedom whatsoever to pursue the things she wanted. And yet, she knew she was falling more in love with him every day.

"Well, I would certainly plan on it being permanent," he said quietly.

The swish of the wipers trying to keep up with the pelting rain filled the small cab of the truck as they rode along.

"But there's my music. . . ."

"You could always commute to the university," he reminded.

". . . and there are all the things in life I want to do."

"We could do them together. There are a lot of places I haven't seen, a lot of things I haven't done. We're young . . . nothing to keep us from exploring new worlds with each other."

"This is all rather sudden on your part, isn't it?" Laurel murmured.

"Sudden? Well, let's see. How old were you the first day you enrolled in grade school here?"

"Around nine, I think."

"Nine? That would have made me around eleven. I'm thirty-three now . . . that's been twenty-two years since I fell in love with you. Yep. This has been a real whirlwind romance."

"Are you serious? You really have been in love with me all these years?"

"Honey, I have loved you so damn long, it's disgusting . . . even to me."

She grinned. "I may have to do something about that one of these days."

"Yes, you just may." He leaned over and kissed her roughly. "And move your hand before I'm forced to cut it off!"

The truck approached a railroad track, and the turkeys began to squabble loudly in the back.

"What's wrong with them now?"Clay adjusted his rearview mirror and tried to see what was causing all the unrest.

Laurel's face turned stormy. "Oh, brother! Just look at that!"

"What?"

"There's a couple of older teenage boys hanging on the back of the truck trying to steal a turkey. They do this all the time."

"Oh, good grief," he said, groaning. "Well, leave them alone. Surely you can spare two turkeys—"

"I certainly will not! The point isn't whether I can spare two turkeys; the point is that they shouldn't be doing things like that. Where are their parents? Imagine letting children their age run around this time of night to steal turkeys. You sit right here. I'll take care of this."

"Laurel!"

But she was out the door before he could stop her. Racing around to the back of the truck, she flew into the unsuspecting boys just as they managed to drag a screaming turkey through the welded cage.

Clay threw on the emergency brakes and jumped out of the truck.

He landed in a mudhole, and his boots sank two feet deep in the grime as he cringed and fought to free himself.

From the back of the truck came feminine screams of rage, the sound of turkeys going crazy, and a couple of boys' voices shouting to grab the turkey and run like the devil.

Clay flinched as the mud came over the top of his boots, and he shouted at Laurel to let the boys go.

But Laurel was possessive of her turkeys and was getting more so by the minute. She picked up a long stick lying beside the shoulder of the road and started beating at the two boys soundly, trying to get them to drop the turkey each had under his arm.

The boys covered their heads with their arms, and the turkeys took off like a shot.

One flew into Clay just as he rounded the truck, nearly knocking him on his back.

"What the hell!"

He staggered backward and grabbed the truck for support as white feathers flew around his head wildly.

"I'll teach you to jump on the back of my turkey trucks and try to take something that isn't yours!" Laurel whacked one of the boys as hard as she could across his rump. "Go home!"

Deciding they would rather give up the turkeys than their lives, the boys broke into a run. Clay reached out and grabbed Laurel around the waist. He held her while she kicked and screamed threats at the two fast-disappearing boys.

"Was that necessary?" he asked in sheer disbelief.

The rain pelted down on them, soaking their clothes as he wrestled her squirming body back to the cab of the truck.

"It certainly was!"

She angrily straightened her clothes and made room for him to get in. When he started the truck, he turned to her and scowled.

"That beats all I've ever seen. You know who you reminded me of back there?"

"Ernestine Raybern." She reached over and plucked two stray turkey feathers out of his dripping hair.

He was staggered that she had read his thoughts so clearly.

"How did you know?"

She shrugged and turned the palms of her hands out guiltily.

"She's my idol now."

The last load of turkeys was delivered shortly after eight o'clock the next morning.

A soft rain was still falling as Laurel and Clay returned to the farmhouse and let themselves in.

Cecile had left a note saying she had gone on to bed. A fresh pot of coffee sat on the stove.

"You want anything to eat?" Laurel yawned as Clay hung up the phone after a brief call.

"No, let's just get some rest," he suggested. "I told Buck I'd be in later on."

He wrapped his arm around her as they slowly climbed the stairs to the bedrooms.

Nothing was mentioned again about his staying with her. It was a foregone conclusion that he would.

Clay paused and took her in his arms to give her a long kiss. They stood on the stairway, sleepily locked in each other's arms, listening to the patter of rain falling on the roof.

"You want the shower first?" Laurel offered.

"Take one with me," he whispered huskily.

Without even a moment's hesitation she accepted his offer. "All right. We'll have to use the bathroom off Dad's room. We'll have complete privacy there."

When they reached the bedroom, Laurel slid the lock on the door into place and walked over to pull the linen shades.

She turned and smiled at him weakly. "I'm afraid that's about all I know. You'll have to take it from here."

"Come here." His voice was deep and resonant. He held out his hand and waited for her to approach him shyly. "You're not afraid, are you?"

"Of you? No."

Laurel thought his hand trembled as he reached out and touched her face reverently. "I dreamed of this moment for twenty-two years, Laurel."

She nodded wordlessly.

"Do you mind if I undress you?"

She shook her head. She didn't care what he did to her . . . only that he was here and wanted her.

"Oh!"

His hand shot back to his side. "What's the matter?"

"I forgot. Do you think I should run down to the drugstore. . .?"

He smiled with relief. He thought she had been about to back out again.

"No, you may not like it, but I took care of things myself this time," he stated firmly.

"That's probably for the best. I'm very inept in that department."

"Well"—his hand moved out to undo the first button of her blouse—"why don't you just leave things like that up to me from now on?"

Her breath caught as he undid the blouse and slipped it off her shoulders. His mouth touched the satin of her shoulders lightly.

"You're pretty good at that," she accused.

"I get better all the time," he murmured.

The snap of her jeans sounded in the quiet room as he continued his work. Moments later the denim fabric joined her blouse on the floor.

For just a brief moment he held her out before him to study her slender frame in the dim light of the room. His eyes turned soft and tender as they ran over every inch of her body, and he moaned.

"Oh, how I love you, Laurel Henderson."

She placed her hands on his cheeks and drew him near to let their mouths touch fleetingly.

"You don't have to keep saying that," she told him, thinking that he felt obligated in view of what was about to take place.

He shook his head wordlessly and buried his face in the auburn silk of her hair. His hands went back to his task as her bra fell away, and then her panties ... and then she was there before him in all her womanly splendor.

She was as lovely as he remembered. His breathing quickened as he reached out to hesitantly touch her creamy softness.

Her eyes watched him trustingly as his hands gently explored her, savoring the feel of her bare skin against the roughness of his hand.

"Are you going to undress?" she asked shyly.

"You want me to?"

Her answer was to begin helping him out of his wet clothes. Seconds later they were pressed against each other as Laurel allowed herself the freedom of learning his body without fear or guilt.

After a moment Clay gently picked her up and carried her to the shower.

The warm water engulfed them as they traded smoldering kisses and tried to bank the growing fires that threatened to consume them before they were both ready.

Clay insisted on washing her.

He couldn't seem to get enough of touching her or tasting her or molding her body tightly against his taut thighs.

He murmured her name over and over again as their kisses grew deeper and longer and more devastating to each other. They were soon locked in a volcano of passion that kept threatening to erupt and overflow and sweep them along in its fiery tide.

The effect he was having on her was shattering, and she found herself urging him to lead her onward onto new paths she had never traveled before.

Laurel wanted to travel those paths with him. There was no longer any doubt that she loved this man beyond her wildest expectations, and she was eager to be his in every way.

In soft words, fleeting touches, and cries of longing, the passion begin to build between them until it was a desire that had to be satisfied.

Clay groaned and shut off the water as his kisses became rough and consuming.

Wrapping her in a large white towel, he carried her to the bed and lay down with her.

"I love you, Laurel," he whispered as he peeled away the towel and once more feasted his eyes on her loveliness.

"Oh, Clay . . . I love you too."

Her soft voice whispering that confession sent his heart soaring, and swift tears sprang to his eyes.

Laurel Henderson—*his* Laurel Henderson— had finally said that she loved him.

"You'll never regret it," he promised as he made ready to claim what he had known all along was rightfully his.

And then, with a gentleness born out of twenty-two years of waiting, Clay Kerwin introduced Laurel Henderson to the act of love.

He took Laurel to places she had only dreamed she would go one day, while she gathered him in her arms and offered him realms of joy he never knew existed.

Together they presented themselves to one another for the sole purpose of love and being loved. When the last mountain was scaled and conquered, they knew that what they had found was perfect.

In the warm afterglow Laurel snuggled in the arms that still held her tightly and thought for a moment that it seemed as if a very important piece of her life's puzzle had suddenly been fitted into place.

She couldn't leave Clay Kerwin.

Without him all the wonderful things out there in that big wide world would quickly lose their flavor.

But could she reconcile herself to never knowing what she had missed?

Before she could give it more thought, Clay's mouth searched for hers once more and all rational thought was put aside.

There would be time to think about that later. . . .

CHAPTER FOURTEEN

The love sated-couple lay tangled in each other's arms among the rumpled bed sheets, chewing bubble gum together and listening to the low rumble of thunder outside.

"Why are we chewing this gum?" Laurel asked in a drowsy voice as she made a feeble attempt to match one of Clay's bubbles.

"I don't know. I suppose it's because I don't smoke anymore." He rolled over, crossing his arms behind his head and proceeded to dazzle her with a monstrous pink orb the size of a grapefruit.

"What do you think of this little beauty?" he lisped, trying to keep it from bursting all over his face.

Laurel made an envious face and stuck the tip of her finger out to poke a hole in the magnificent sphere.

The bubble collapsed in a pink, sticky glob all over his face.

"Oh, now, come on!" He sat up and began pulling at the pink strings dripping off his face

"That's what you get for showing off," she admonished, laughing.

His stern blue eyes bore into hers solemnly. "Ugh. Chew squaw in hot water with big Chief now. She made him look like gummy fool."

"He *is* gummy fool." She grinned and kissed the tip of his nose.

They both worked at getting his face clean again before he took her in his arms and hugged her tightly. His hand caressed her bare bottom absently as he leaned up on one elbow to gaze at her.

"Lady, you have made me the happiest man in the world this morning," he whispered.

"Thank you, sir. You weren't too shabby yourself."

Her smile was as intimate as their kisses had been. Their eyes met tenderly as he gently eased her back on the pillow and his lips recaptured hers.

It was several long moments later before Clay groaned and pulled away from her. "We have to stop this," he begged. "It's getting close to noon, and I have to get to the office."

"But, Clay," she protested, "you haven't been to sleep all night. You're exhausted."

"That can't be helped." He peered at his watch and tried to make out the time in the dim light. "Buck's been covering for me down at the jail, and I promised I'd get there as soon as I could. I think my watch has stopped."

"I heard you talking to him on the phone this

morning. Did those two men confess who they were working for?"

He pretended to be preoccupied with his watch.

The two men had indeed confessed to being responsible for the vandalism over the last few weeks.

And it hadn't taken very long for Buck to persuade them to confess who had been paying their salary. It was the person Clay had feared all along.

But he just didn't have the heart to tell her . . . at least not yet.

He wanted the culprit safely locked away before he broke the news.

Then he would take her in his arms and try to heal the deep hurt she would undoubtedly feel.

"Didn't I see a clock on the bedside table?" he asked evasively, leaning over to search for the illuminated clock. His hand fumbled around blindly. By accident his hand hit the old family bible next to the clock and knocked it to the floor.

Laurel slid out of bed and reached for her towel. She leaned down and began to pick up the scattered papers that had fallen out of the bible.

"Doggone it. It's later than I thought," Clay grumbled, seeing the time. He swung his long legs out of bed and reached for his pants.

Rearranging the papers neatly back in order, Laurel paused as she came across a scrap of napkin stuck away in the front of the worn pages.

Sam had spent many hours of his last days reading the bible he had tried so hard to live by. Laurel picked up the napkin, startled to recognize her father's handwriting scrawled weakly across the flimsy paper.

"Honey? Is there something wrong?" Clay sat down on the bed and switched on the bedside lamp.

"I don't know. This piece of paper fell out of Sam's bible," she said. "There's something written on it in his handwriting."

She sat down on the bed next to Clay and moved the paper closer to the light.

"I'm sorry, Cecile," it read. "Forgive a bitter old man. Laurel will take care of you. I love you both."

"Oh, Clay." Laurel's eyes filled with grateful tears. "Dad must have written this just before he passed away. Cecile will be so happy."

"He knew his daughters well." Clay smiled, his love for her shining in the depths of his blue eyes. "One was a little mixed up and needed time to get her life back in order. But he knew the other one had her head screwed on right and would be there waiting when the black sheep came back home."

Laurel knew as well as Clay that Sam had not meant the treasured note for Cecile alone.

The silent message he was handing down from

the heavens was a simple one: Sam Henderson wanted the farm, and all his earthly possessions, split equally between his two daughters . . . something Laurel had done weeks ago, anyway.

Confusion and pain clouded Laurel's face as it suddenly occurred to her that if Cecile *had* been part of all the trouble Laurel had experienced lately, it had all been in vain.

Her troubled eyes found Clay's. She knew he had the name of her persecutor in his possession and had only been waiting for the right time to tell her.

"Please . . . is it Cecile?" she begged, willing him to tell her it wasn't so.

Clay's face was grave as he shook his head. "No. Dan and Cecile have fallen in love with each other, nothing more. They just didn't want to say anything to anyone until they were sure. Dan has told me he wants to marry your sister as soon as possible."

A heavy weight was lifted from Laurel's heart. She was so happy that two fine people had found each other. But, if it wasn't them . . .

"Then it's the Rowden boys? I thought that's who it was all along."

"No, not the Rowden boys, either," he dismissed. "The night Cecile saw them over here they were simply stealing your turkeys, not sabotaging them."

"Stealing my turkeys! Why, those . . ." She paused, and her face clouded with confusion. "If it wasn't Dan and Cecile or the Rowden

270

boys, then who has been trying to run me out of business?"

The bedroom door suddenly burst open. Clay and Laurel snapped their heads around to face the intruder.

Laurel's face clouded with shock and disbelief. At the door stood a white-faced Cecile pressed tightly against Paige Moyer's side, a gun jammed in her ribs.

"Oh, no ... not you, Paige," Laurel whispered brokenly.

"Get your clothes on, Laurel," Paige ordered calmly. "You're coming with me."

Clay moved for the gun in the holster he had dropped on the chair last night, but he wasn't fast enough.

Paige waved his gun menacingly in Clay's direction.

"Stay right where you are, Clay. I don't want to shoot you, but I will."

"Paige, you son of a bitch, you touch one hair on her head and I won't be responsible for what I do to you," Clay warned in a deadly tone. His eyes burned blue-hot coals in the lawyer's direction as he watched Paige warily.

"I'm not afraid of you, Sheriff," Paige returned evenly. He moved the barrel of the gun over in Laurel's direction once more. "I said, get dressed."

Laurel glanced at Clay anxiously.

"Do what he says, sweetheart. He's a sick man."

"I don't have any clothes in here," she whispered fearfully.

Cecile handed her a bundle of clothes she had in her hand. "Here . . . I brought these for you." She gave her sister a shaky smile but looked faint with fear.

"Are you all right?" Laurel asked, dragging on the clothes with trembling hands.

Cecile could only nod wordlessly.

"Paige, don't do this," Clay said, trying to reason with the wild-eyed man standing in the doorway. "There is no money buried anywhere on this land," he stated bluntly. "You're a sick man and need help. Let us help you, Paige." He held out his hand for the gun, and Paige stepped back a few feet.

"Oh, but you're wrong, Clay. There are thousands of dollars buried right here near the house," he estimated wildly, his voice rising to a frenzied pitch.

Laurel stared at the man who had been like a father to her over the years and fought to make sense out of what he was saying.

Money! Buried on her land? What in the world was he talking about?

"There isn't one red cent buried here," Clay snapped. "It's all in your mind, Paige, a figment of your imagination."

Clay began to ease off the bed, but Paige stopped him abruptly.

"Stay where you are! I mean it!"

"What is he talking about, Clay?" Laurel turned pleading eyes in his direction, seeking an answer to this madness.

"I didn't know how to tell you, honey. After

talking to several people around town, Buck and I found out that Paige has it in his head that his grandparents buried a staggering amount of money somewhere on this property."

"They did," Paige shouted. "And it's all mine when I find it!"

Clay turned to look at him sadly. "Paige, your grandparents never owned this land. I've been through every land-sale record in the county since they began keeping journals. And there is no log of your family ever owning anything even remotely near here. They lived on five acres over on the other side of the river that wasn't good for anything but raising rocks. From what I could find out they were barely able to keep food on their table, let alone bury a fortune."

"You're wrong," he stated emphatically, stomping his foot in a childish gesture. "My grandparents owned this land and hundreds of head of cattle and raised soybeans and wheat.... They worked all their lives for that money, and I have a map that shows it's buried right here next to the cellar!"

Paige was becoming more irate as he shoved Cecile farther into the room, waiting for Laurel to finish dressing. "It's mine, and no one is going to take it away from me," he whined. "My grandparents worked hard all their lives. They would want me to have that money. When I find it, I'm going to be able to do all the things they never got to do," he reasoned childishly. "They would want that." He seemed to drift off in a demented, private world all his own.

"But, Paige," Laurel spoke softly. "You don't need money. You've had a good business all these years ... you never married or had children. You're bound to be a rich man in your own right."

"He is, Laurel." Clay's deep voice filled the tense room. "But greed for more has stolen his mind. Apparently Paige has been hurtling toward a mental breakdown for the last few months, but he wouldn't accept anyone's help."

Laurel had been aware of his strange moods recently, but she had never dreamed it was anything this serious.

Oh, he had been forgetful and a little quick to lose his temper, but like everyone else, she had attributed his actions to old age and approaching senility.

"But why does he want to hurt me?" she pleaded.

"I don't think he really does, but in his muddled mind he thinks that if he can get you and Cecile out of the way, he can get his hands on the money."

"But that's ... sick! Now that you know he's crazy, it wouldn't do any good for him to harm us. ..."

Paige stood watching them talk, his face remaining expressionless as Cecile trembled in his arms.

Clay's face filled with despair. "He's sick, Laurel. He doesn't know what he's doing."

"I think he finally snapped when he found

out I wanted us to keep the farm," Cecile offered weakly.

Laurel's heart begin to hammer with dread. "My gosh, Clay. Is he really going to try to . . . hurt us?" Her voice broke off fearfully. Who knew what was going on in his twisted mind right now.

"He'll have to kill me first," Clay promised grimly.

"No, Clay." Laurel knew he meant every word he said, and she couldn't bear the thought of anything happening to him. Surely, when it came right down to it, Paige would not hurt her or Cecile. She would far rather take her chances with Paige than risk losing Clay.

Paige smiled at Laurel benevolently. "It's time to go now, dear. I want you to take this rope and tie Clay to the bed." He threw the rope he had been holding in his hand in Laurel's direction. "I don't want to hurt him, but I will if he forces me to."

Laurel's good intentions melted in the face of reality, and she started backing away in fright. "No, Paige . . ."

"You must obey me, dear." He pulled Cecile closer and leveled the barrel of the gun to her temple.

Laurel couldn't do anything but obey. With trembling hands she walked over to Clay. "You'll have to lie down so I can tie your hands," she murmured.

Clay lay back and let her fasten his hands to

the bedpost. "Don't worry, honey. I'll take care of you," he whispered.

For a moment she faltered. Leaning toward him, she buried her face in his neck. "Oh, Clay. I'm so scared," she whimpered.

"I love you, Laurel. Trust me." His voice sounded as shaky as hers, but she did trust him. She had to.

She smothered a sob as she finished her task and turned to face Paige. He walked over to check the bindings, then motioned to her.

"Come, dear. You don't need to be afraid. I have to do this, don't you see?" He looked at her benignly. "It's what my grandparents want."

"Leave her alone, Paige." Clay growled another sober warning from his place on the bed.

"Now, Laurel." Paige pointed the gun at her and waited.

As if in a trance, Laurel moved over next to Cecile. Paige reached out and shoved them into the hallway.

"I'm warning you, Paige. Don't you lay a hand on either one of them!" Laurel could hear Clay's voice angrily shouting at Paige as he steered them through the empty house.

Cecile wrapped her arms around her sister and hugged her close as they stumbled out the back door. When they reached the farmyard Paige shoved them both in the backseat of his car and took the driver's seat.

Cecile peered out the window looking for Dan in desperation, but her eyes failed to spot him as the car careened wildly out of the drive and onto the highway.

"This is what they would want," Paige kept reminding himself as the car picked up speed. "They would want me to have their money. I don't want to hurt you, Laurel, but I have to . . . don't you see? If you had only sold me the farm and gone on with your music instead of making a new will and listening to Cecile . . . why, everything would be fine right now. You've forced me into doing this," he accused petulantly. "You shouldn't have listened to Cecile. She always was the wild one. She didn't want the farm, I did. . . ."

Paige rattled on and on as the rain started to pelt down on the windshield once more.

"I'll have to take you out here somewhere and . . . well, I don't know what I'll do. I'm afraid I'll probably . . . But it will be over quickly," he promised. "I wouldn't let my little girl suffer." He gave a demented laugh and pushed down harder on the gas pedal.

Laurel stared blankly ahead of her, her mind still back in the room with Clay.

He had looked so helpless lying there on the bed. What could he possibly do to save her now? The answer she came up with was chilling. Absolutely nothing.

Where was all the happiness they had shared only a few hours ago? During that precious time she had realized that she wanted to marry Clay more than she wanted her freedom. With Clay's love she would be free, free to spend the rest of her life discovering this big wide world with him. Would she ever have that chance now, or would Paige end that hope for her?

Clay must save her. He had to save her, she thought as the car hurtled down the highway.

Hurry, Clay. Hurry, Clay. Hurry, darling.

She wanted to know the joy of living her life with him. The haunting blue of his eyes came back to torment her as she remembered what he'd told her just that morning as they were making love.

"You are my only love, Laurel," he had whispered reverently. "From the first day we met I knew you were destined to be mine."

Laurel could hear Cecile sobbing quietly beside her as the car continued to pick up speed.

We're all going to be killed, Laurel thought helplessly as the car swerved nearly out of control on a curve.

Paige was driving like a maniac on this wet pavement, and she knew he was lost in a world all his own . . . where no one could reach him.

The car skidded again as she heard the faint wail of a siren coming from behind them. Paige glanced in the rearview mirror and saw Clay's patrol car gaining on him. Pressing down harder on the accelerator, he laughed like a crazed devil.

"You'll never stop me," he shouted gleefully. "Grandma! Can you hear me? I'm coming to visit you, Grandma. I'm coming!"

The car lurched wildly, skidding off the road

toward a steep ravine. Laurel closed her eyes, clutching on to Cecile's hand.

Unhindered by trees, the car rolled down the ravine, tossing its occupants about like rag dolls.

Cecile's screams filled Laurel's ears as she tried to hold on to her sister but failed.

The taste of blood filled Laurel's mouth as she was slammed and thrown around the car. She felt the bone in her arm snap just before the car came to rest on its side.

For a moment there was only the sound of glass breaking and the smell of gas choking the air.

Laurel glanced around her, trying to see if there were any pearly gates in sight, but her eyes filled with the rain that was coming down in a steady torrent. She closed her eyes again.

The sounds of shouts and someone running down the hillside barely registered in her confused mind as she fought to remain conscious.

Cecile?

Her hands searched frantically for her sister, but to her surprise, she found she was no longer in the car.

Laurel was lying on the ground in a puddle of muddy water, thrown clear of the wreckage. Her eyes focused on a small form lying twenty feet away.

"Cecile, can you hear me?" she called weakly.

She couldn't be dead. Not before Laurel explained how sorry she was for what she had been thinking the last few weeks . . . not before she told her about Sam leaving the new will in his bible.

"I'm sorry. . . ." Hot tears streamed from Laurel's eyes as she tried to pour out her apology.

She had no idea if Cecile could hear her, but it didn't matter. She had to confess.

"I thought it was you and Dan trying to take the farm. I didn't know that you loved Dan until Clay told me this morning. And Sam . . . he left a new will in his bible stating he loved you and wanted you to share half of his estate. Oh, Cecile, I've been so wrong about so many things!" A broken sob interrupted her stream of frenzied words. "All I've ever really wanted out of life was to enjoy my music and have someone to love me the way Clay does. When this is all over, I'm going to let you and Dan have the farm. You two deserve happiness. Please . . . can you ever forgive me for doubting you?"

From the spot where she lay, Cecile moaned and said crossly, "Can we talk about this another time?"

Laurel wanted to laugh. She felt so much relief that her sister was alive and had heard her heartfelt confession, but it hurt too much. "Are you all right?"

"No. I think every bone in my body's broken. But I'm alive," she murmured gratefully. "How about you?"

"My arm's broken," Laurel reported. Hot tears of relief streamed down her cheeks as she thought of Clay once more. Maybe now there *would* be a future with him. "What about Paige?" Laurel asked.

"I don't know. I can't see him. Can you?"

Laurel turned carefully, and her eyes fastened on the twisted body of Paige still in the wreckage of the car. "He's in the car. I don't know if he's alive or not."

All of a sudden there was a loud explosion as the car burst into flames. Seconds later two men came running from the road. Stumbling through the underbrush along the ravine, they hurriedly surveyed the chaos.

Laurel blinked hard as she tried to bring the figures of the men into focus.

"Laurel!" she heard one of them shout frantically.

"Here . . . I'm over here," she called dazedly.

Clay's head spun around and he started toward her in long strides.

Seconds later she was lifted in his strong arms and carried hurriedly away from the burning wreckage.

"Paige is still in there. . . ." she murmured.

"I'll get him. There's an ambulance on the way." He groaned and kissed her possessively. "When this is all over, I'm never going to let you out of my sight," he promised, laying her carefully on the ground.

She watched as he ran back over to the burning wreckage and disappeared inside. Holding her breath, she let out a sigh of relief when he came back into view carrying Paige.

"Laurel, dear," Paige was moaning. "I'm sorry

. . . so sorry. I didn't mean to hurt you. Laurel . . . is she hurt?"

"Take it easy, Paige. Laurel is going to be fine," Clay assured gruffly. "And we're going to get you the help you need."

"Thank you, Clay. You're a fine man . . . fine man. You take good care of my little girl. You will, won't you?" He clutched the front of Clay's shirt tightly.

"I will. You can count on it."

"I love her like she was my own little girl," he muttered. "My own little girl. I didn't want to hurt her. Tell her I didn't mean to hurt her. . . ."

The medics came over and relieved Clay of his burden. Seconds later he was back at Laurel's side.

"Oh, Laurel . . . oh, Laurel." He kept repeating her name as he showered soft kisses around her mouth. Carefully he ran his hands over every square inch of her, checking for injuries.

"Clay, you pick the darnedest times to make a pass at a girl!" she scolded feebly, echoing the words he had once teased her with.

"Lie still, honey," he cautioned tenderly.

"Clay?"

"Shhh . . ."

He cradled her head in his lap, fighting the urge to take her in his arms and hug her until they were both senseless. Unsure of the extent of her injuries, he settled for bringing his mouth down to touch hers gently once more.

"Oh, Laurel, honey . . . I thought I had lost you."

His salty tears mingled with hers now as they kissed over and over.

She moaned as pain shot through her arm.

"Where's the damn ambulance!" he shouted to Dan, who was giving Cecile the same tender loving care Clay was bestowing on Laurel.

"It's on its way," Dan called back.

For the first time since she had left him tied to the bed in her father's room, Laurel began to realize that Clay was sitting here beside her, tears streaming down his face.

Her hand wrapped around his wet head, and she pulled him against her chest with her one good arm.

"I knew you would come," she said, sobbing. "But how did you get away? I tied the rope so tight!"

"Are you kidding?" he scoffed. "I was out of those ropes before you left the driveway." He tenderly kissed her again. "Dan came driving in just a few minutes after you left, and we followed you all the way. Oh, honey"—his eyes grew painful—"I've never been so scared in all my life. I felt so helpless, so powerless to stop what was happening."

"It doesn't matter now. It's all over," Laurel said, soothing him and showering him with loving kisses.

Suddenly his face turned solemn. He held her away from him so that he could gaze lovingly into her eyes. "Honey . . . listen to me. I know this is a bad time to bring this up, but a few minutes ago when I thought I was going to lose you, I nearly went out of my mind. Laurel, if you'll marry me, I'll see that you go on with your music. I'll allow you all the freedom you could ever dream of, and together we'll travel to the ends of the earth . . . just you and me, honey." His beautiful eyes clouded with fresh tears as Laurel reached up to gently touch his face. "I want you, Laurel. I always have," he finished raggedly.

The wail of sirens filled the air. In the distance came loud rumbles of thunder as Laurel gazed back at Clay with complete adoration. "I want you too."

His smile was heartwarming. "Then you will marry me?"

At that moment paramedics interrupted the two lovers as they moved to examine Laurel and place her on a stretcher.

Dan came over while they were strapping Laurel down. He told them he was going to ride in the ambulance with Cecile. Like Paige, her injuries were numerous, but they would both recover completely.

"Hey."

Laurel glanced over to see Clay walking next to her. She was starting to grow drowsy from the shot she had been given for pain. "What?" she whispered.

He lifted his hand up to his nose and made a "bill." Wiggling it playfully, he winked at her. "Will you marry me?"

Her good hand went weakly to her bottom and made the imaginary tail he was so fond of—not a good one, but it was the best she could do at the moment.

She wiggled it weakly and smiled back at him. "I certainly will."

His face was as radiant as the sun peeping over the hill on a fine summer morning. "Soon?"

"Well, I might be out of circulation for a few days," she noted sleepily. "But as soon as I can."

"Great!" The elation that filled his voice boomed over the rainy hillside as the paramedics began the long climb back up the ravine with their patient. "Maybe next week?" he prompted.

Laurel had to laugh. "Maybe." She closed her eyes, but seconds later they popped back open. "Oh, Clay. Can I let Cecile and Dan have the turkeys?"

"Are you serious? I can't think of anything I'd like better!" His voice was getting farther away now as she drew closer to unconsciousness.

"You know, it's going to be nice married to you," she said dreamily. "I'll bake you gooseberry pies anytime you want."

Clay glanced over at the paramedics and grinned lamely. "I've been meaning to talk to you about that, honey. I'm getting kind of tired of gooseberry. How about . . . cherry for a change?"

"Cherry? But I thought your favorite was gooseberry?"

"Oh it is . . . was. I've just sort of burned

myself out on it," he said casually. "I'm into cherry now."

"Well, whatever you want," she conceded. She could feel herself drifting off fast. "But I had a new recipe I wanted to try. It's a stuffing that calls for apples, but I thought I could use gooseberries. . . ." Her voice fell silent as the medicine took full control.

As the attendants closed the ambulance doors, Clay let out one tired sigh.

Whatever he wanted?

He didn't want anything. He had it all. He had his Laurel Henderson, and that's all he had *ever* wanted.

COMING IN JANUARY!
TIMESWEPT ROMANCE

TIME OF THE ROSE
By Bonita Clifton

When the silver-haired cowboy brings Madison Calloway to his run-down ranch, she thinks for sure he is senile. Certain he'll bring harm to himself, Madison follows the man into a thunderstorm and back to the wild days of his youth in the Old West.

The dread of all his enemies and the desire of all the ladies, Colton Chase does not stand a chance against the spunky beauty who has tracked him through time. And after one passion-drenched night, Colt is ready to surrender his heart to the most tempting spitfire anywhere in time.

_51922-4 $4.99 US/$5.99 CAN

A FUTURISTIC ROMANCE

AWAKENINGS
By Saranne Dawson

Fearless and bold, Justan rules his domain with an iron hand, but nothing short of the Dammai's magic will bring his warring people peace. He claims he needs Rozlynd—a bewitching beauty and the last of the Dammai—for her sorcery alone, yet inside him stirs an unexpected yearning to savor the temptress's charms, to sample her sweet innocence. And as her silken spell ensnares him, Justan battles to vanquish a power whose like he has never encountered—the power of Rozlynd's love.

_51921-6 $4.99 US/$5.99 CAN

FROM LOVE SPELL
FUTURISTIC ROMANCE
NO OTHER LOVE
Flora Speer
Bestselling Author of *A Time To Love Again*

Only Herne sees the woman. To the other explorers of the ruined city she remains unseen, unknown. But after an illicit joining she is gone, and Herne finds he cannot forget his beautiful seductress, or ignore her uncanny resemblance to another member of the exploration party. Determined to unravel the puzzle, Herne begins a seduction of his own—one that will unleash a whirlwind of danger and desire.

_51916-X $4.99 US/$5.99 CAN

TIMESWEPT ROMANCE
LOVE'S TIMELESS DANCE
Vivian Knight-Jenkins

Although the pressure from her company's upcoming show is driving Leeanne Sullivan crazy, she refuses to believe she can be dancing in her studio one minute—and with a seventeenth-century Highlander the next. A liberated woman like Leeanne will have no problem teaching virile Iain MacBride a new step or two, and soon she'll have him begging for lessons in love.

_51917-8 $4.99 US/$5.99 CAN

LOVE SPELL
ATTN: Order Department
Dorchester Publishing Company, Inc.
276 5th Avenue, New York, NY 10001

Please add $1.50 for shipping and handling for the first book and $.35 for each book thereafter. PA., N.Y.S. and N.Y.C. residents, please add appropriate sales tax. No cash, stamps, or C.O.D.s. All orders shipped within 6 weeks via postal service book rate. Canadian orders require $2.00 extra postage and must be paid in U.S. dollars through a U.S. banking facility.

Name _____

Address _____

City _____ State _____ Zip _____

I have enclosed $_____ in payment for the checked book(s).

Payment <u>must</u> accompany all orders.□ Please send a free catalog.

FROM LOVE SPELL
HISTORICAL ROMANCE
THE PASSIONATE REBEL
Helene Lehr

A beautiful American patriot, Gillian Winthrop is horrified to learn that her grandmother means her to wed a traitor to the American Revolution. Her body yearns for Philip Meredith's masterful touch, but she is determined not to give her hand—or any other part of herself—to the handsome Tory, until he convinces her that he too is a passionate rebel.

__51918-6 $4.99 US/$5.99 CAN

CONTEMPORARY ROMANCE
THE TAWNY GOLD MAN
Amii Lorin

Bestselling Author Of More Than 5 Million Books In Print!

Long ago, in a moment of wild, rioting ecstasy, Jud Cammeron vowed to love her always. Now, as Anne Moore looks at her stepbrother, she sees a total stranger, a man who plans to take control of his father's estate and everyone on it. Anne knows things are different—she is a grown woman with a fiance—but something tells her she still belongs to the tawny gold man.

__51919-4 $4.99 US/$5.99 CAN

LOVE SPELL
ATTN: Order Department
Dorchester Publishing Company, Inc.
276 5th Avenue, New York, NY 10001

Please add $1.50 for shipping and handling for the first book and $.35 for each book thereafter. PA., N.Y.S. and N.Y.C. residents, please add appropriate sales tax. No cash, stamps, or C.O.D.s. All orders shipped within 6 weeks via postal service book rate. Canadian orders require $2.00 extra postage and must be paid in U.S. dollars through a U.S. banking facility.

Name _____

Address _____

City _____ State _____ Zip _____

I have enclosed $_____in payment for the checked book(s). Payment <u>must</u> accompany all orders.☐ Please send a free catalog.

AN HISTORICAL ROMANCE
GILDED SPLENDOR
By Elizabeth Parker

Bound for the London stage, sheltered Amanda Prescott has no idea that fate has already cast her first role as a rakehell's true love. But while visiting Patrick Winter's country estate, she succumbs to the dashing peer's burning desire. Amid the glittering milieu of wealth and glamour, Amanda and Patrick banish forever their harsh past and make all their fantasies a passionate reality.

__51914-3 $4.99 US/$5.99 CAN

A CONTEMPORARY ROMANCE
MADE FOR EACH OTHER/RAVISHED
By Parris Afton Bonds
Bestselling Author of *The Captive*

In *Made for Each Other,* reporter Julie Dever thinks she knows everything about Senator Nicholas Raffer—until he rescues her from a car wreck and shares with her a passion she never dared hope for. And in *Ravished*, a Mexican vacation changes nurse Nelli Walzchak's life when she is kidnapped by a handsome stranger who needs more than her professional help.

__51915-1 $4.99 US/$5.99 CAN